the
boardwalk
house

an heirloom island novel

ELIZABETH
BROMKE

Created with Vellum

PROLOGUE

Water kissed the shoreline gently on Heirloom Island. Crystalline blue surf trickled up beach sand and met with a thatch of green grass.

That's where Darla stood now, unsure if she preferred the sandy beach or the grass that spread so pervasively across all Michigan towns.

Lake Huron—well, the Great Lakes in general—were different that way. Sure, they promised all the usual things that an ocean's beach did: tides and wakes, surf and sand. But there was more to a Great Lake than what a beachgoer may expect.

That was the special thing about Heirloom Island and Birch Harbor and all those Michigan towns that kept themselves secret from the rest of the world. Sparkling blue water. Private docks that stretched over green lawns onto the lake and into the horizon. Beauty on a grand scale.

It wasn't, however, the beauty that made her setting special.

In fact, such specialness came down to the element of surprise. Bright lakeside surprise.

When Darla arrived here those few days ago, the beauty was a given. Something to take for granted. Of course it was beautiful, it was an island. Of course the trip was lovely, it was a vacation.

Then, everything changed. Overnight, it had changed.

Although, if Darla had been paying closer attention, the change wasn't overnight. It was gradual. So gradual that it hit her like a ton of bricks. That she'd needed someone else—her sister—to point it out. To *see* it. To see the truth.

Presently, she pressed her hands against her torso, breathing deeply to a five-count. In for five. Out for five. The water ebbed and flowed with her, shifting out and in. Out and in.

A laugh crawled up the back of Darla's throat, but it came out more like a sob. Funny, how life could go. Sad, too. Mainly, though, life was nothing if not unexpected. Much like Lake Huron and Heirloom Island, the sliver of land floating like a chunk of golf course turf chipped up, loose, misplaced.

She sucked in a final, longer breath. An uncountable breath. She blew it out across the water then turned to face the boardwalk house, a Cape Cod type of thing that glowed under the milky, star-strewn night sky.

It occurred to her that places like this, like the board-walk on Heirloom Island, were something of a secret. A secret that belonged to family. To the town. To Michigan...to *Earth* herself.

Darla had secrets, as well. Two, to be exact. At least, two that mattered.

One, she hoped would solve itself. Never to be revealed. The sort of secret that could disappear on a dew drop, slipping down into the fertile soil of Heirloom Island, never to see the light of day again.

The other, well, she was about to bare it all.

To her sisters. In the boardwalk house.

Right now.

1

ONE MONTH EARLIER

You're horrible.

The insult continued to ring in Darla Sage-berry's mind long after Hunter had left.

In some ways, she *was* horrible. What kind of person broke up with her intended just a month from their big day? Only horrible people did that.

So, she deserved the verbal slap. It numbed her, but she deserved it. And what made her even more horrible was just how easily she had ended things.

Two years of dating, six months of engagement, one trip to the courthouse, and once she'd made up her mind, it was all over. Like a razor blade through warm butter.

She'd practiced. For days—maybe even weeks—she'd practiced in her head.

I'm just not ready was the first iteration.

Something feels wrong, don't you agree? was the second.

The third, and final, *I can't do this, Hunter. I'm so sorry, but it's over.*

A dagger to his heart, and she was to blame.

He hadn't taken it well, clearly. He fumed. His nostrils flared. His cheeks flushed neon red. His voice even rose, attracting humiliating attention from the other tables at the coffee shop. Of course, it was during this public tantrum that she was proved right in her estimation that a marriage to Hunter S. James would never work. His temper aside, he couldn't just stop and ask her *Why?*

Maybe, if he had, he'd still be there with her. They'd work it out. Maybe delay the reception, but they'd be together.

Of course, he didn't ask. He just raged, and, therefore, horrible she would be. Darla accepted this. Because, of course, being horrible was far preferable to being whatever she'd have become had she stayed with him.

"Can I get you anything?" a flitting barista asked too chirpily.

Darla forced a smile and shook her head. In reality, she needed lots of things. She needed to call someone, first. To scream across the phone that *she did it!* Triumphant and happy, she *did* it. But even her closest friend—her sister Tatum—would pity Hunter, not Darla. Hunter was the wounded one. Darla the perpetrator. Despite his defects, he'd come out the sorry sack and she, well, the horrible one.

Once she was alone again, Darla did pull out her phone. Instead of a call, she shot off that text to Tatum. The same *I did it* that buzzed in her head, but now flatter. Muted, since it was a text. No number of exclamation marks or smiley faces would reflect the thrill in her voice.

After, she shoved her phone deep into her purse and

emerged with her day planner. A small, floral-patterned thing that was almost halfway used.

May in Michigan was beautiful, and it finally felt like her chosen pattern made sense. Back on December 26, when Darla had selected it from a paltry shelf of clearance organizational supplies, she was more tempted to go with the white one. White with red cardinals speckled across the cover. But she knew eventually flowers would bloom. Now, maybe they were blooming.

With a pen in hand, Darla flipped first to today's date. She clicked the barrel into position and hovered over her to-do list.

Not on that list was breaking up with Hunter.

That was the sort of to-do that a gal didn't document in ink. It was the kind that dwelled in her head and her heart, eating away like a parasite.

What she *had* documented was a second wedding dress fitting. Now, instead of suffering a three-way mirror and pins and tucks, she could relax. What a relief.

She drew a straight line through that item, then beneath it wrote *Cancel*.

The next days and weeks were filled with similar obligations. Obligations for which she'd still have to pay, or at least lose the deposit. Ones Darla would miss, no doubt. Maybe she'd never get another chance at them.

Maybe she would.

Instead of reviewing the rest of the day's tasks or adding new ones, such as a sad visit to the county courthouse to undo what she and Hunter had already set in motion, Darla paged to the far back of her planner. The notes section, where she kept a different sort of to-do list.

Her bucket list.

Year by year, along with birthdays and reminders to schedule various doctors' visits, Darla would painstakingly copy her ten-item list into the next planner. And the next after that. It was a list she'd devised ten years earlier, at the tender age of twenty-five.

When she was twenty-five, her age felt anything but tender. It felt empty and unpredictable, volatile, even. Some things never changed.

Funnier still, that of her ten-item bucket list, she'd accomplished just one item. Staring at it, she was startled when her phone vibrated audibly from the depths of her purse.

She expected it to be Tatum, feverish with excitement and condolences and desperate to know how the breakup went.

It was not Tatum, however.

It was the last person in the world Darla wanted to talk to.

"I'M SO SORRY, DARLA." Cadence churned her words until they came out like cream, smooth and fluid and as sincere as she could possibly make them. The last time she'd chatted on the phone with her younger sister was six months earlier, when Darla dared to call with news of her engagement. Not a text or email or anything else since. Save for the wedding invitation.

As soon as Cadence had received Tatum's message—
It's off!—Cadence flew to her refrigerator and plucked the

ivory rectangle of cardstock out from its magnet, tore it in two, and dropped it in the trash.

Soon thereafter, she wrapped herself in a black silk kimono and traipsed to the deck. It was there, in her wicker chaise with its cream-colored padding, that she tapped her phone back to life and put the call through.

It caught her off guard that Darla answered at all.

"Cadence?" Darla seemed confused.

"Yes. I—well, Tatum told me what happened," Cadence murmured back, her voice low. "Are you okay? Tatum said she's heading your way now. You shouldn't be alone, Darla."

What did Cadence know about breakups? Maybe the very thing Darla needed was to be alone. This situation wasn't like Cadence's. Hunter didn't die. Darla wasn't a widow.

"I'm okay, and I haven't technically talked to Tatum yet." A sarcastic, mirthless chuckle rippled over the connection.

Cadence frowned. "You aren't okay."

"No, no!" Darla's voice brightened. "I really am. It's just funny how quickly bad news travels."

"Bad news?" Cadence cocked an eyebrow and studied her bare fingernails. She hadn't gotten a manicure since Hendrik's passing. Going on eleven months. In one more month, she'd resume normal activity. Stop wearing black. Appear again in public. The whole nine.

Darla snorted on the other end. "To most people, it is bad news. The cancellation of a wedding brings out the heartache in would-be wedding guests, I suppose."

Cadence chewed her lip. If only Darla's supposition

were true. But that was a generalization. Not all weddings were created equal. Not all marriages, either.

She sighed. "Anyway, good or bad, it's hard, I'd imagine." Right? Surely, it must be. All that preparation. That hope. Down the drain, pearls and all.

"It'll be harder in a month," Darla answered, "when I have to be out of my apartment."

Cadence winced for her sister. "Your lease is up? Can't you sign for another year?" More to the point, would she *want* to? At thirty-five years old, surely Darla had outgrown a one-bedroom apartment near the university.

"No. I dug my own grave with this one. Seriously." Darla paused on the other end, and Cadence wondered if it was because here they were, two regular sisters having a regular conversation. As if nothing was wrong between them. She gave Darla another beat to explain. It worked. "I set up a contract for the girl who's taking my place. It's a done deal. There won't be other vacancies here come June. And if I'm not living here, I'll need to get another job."

"Why?" Cadence prodded gently.

"The discount I get for managing the complex is steep. Half off. I can't afford to stay here at my current paycheck, though."

Biting her tongue, Cadence knew better than to point out the obvious. Staying with Hunter would have been the easy path. With his salary alone, they'd share a pretty two-story in the suburbs. She'd be a plump, happy housewife had she married him. Just like Cadence had become. Except Darla would be even better off. Not because Hunter made more money, but for *other* reasons. *Social* reasons. No one would have questioned their union. No one would have batted an eye.

"Will you keep your position with the university?" Cadence asked, trying to keep the conversation afloat, productive.

Darla hummed on the other end, as if this were up for negotiation. At last, she answered, "It's just an adjunct gig. I'm part-time. No tenure, of course. Nothing really tying me."

"Have you signed a contract for next school year?" Teacher language—even professor language—was a common thread between the sisters. Perhaps the only common thread now. Now that Darla would not marry. At least, not yet.

"It's not due until the end of the month. I had been... waiting to see what happened. Maybe I wouldn't be able to keep teaching, you know."

"Hm. Right. Well, I'm sure things will work themselves out." Cadence's jaw clenched. She'd love to offer her sister a refuge. Really, she would, but... "Darla, you shouldn't be alone, okay? Stay with Tatum. Or Mom. Promise me."

Darla hesitated only momentarily before thanking Cadence tightly then ending the call.

Maybe she did want to be alone.

Maybe Cadence was wrong after all.

After the call, as Cadence stretched deep into her chaise and watched early-season boaters dare the frigid waters, she thought about what Darla said. That she was *waiting* to sign her contract. Waiting to decide about life. Waiting to *see what happened*.

Cadence knew exactly what Darla had been waiting for. The same thing that Cadence had waited for. The same thing that any young bride—or even not-so-young bride—waited for.

The promise of a baby.

Of course, with no imminent wedding, there would be no baby. There would be no reason in the world *not* to stay at the university, *not* to sign the contract.

Not to upend her entire life.

"YOU JUST WANTED *CHILDREN*." Tatum let the word fall out like a wet toad flopping in mud. Darla was in her apartment, her arms and head sprawling on the kitchen table in a dramatic show of—what? Regret?

"Yeah," Darla mumbled back. "I mean, I still do. That's why I stuck with him. I'm of advanced maternal age, you know."

Tatum lifted an eyebrow. "So?"

"Having kids at this point could be...complicated. Or even impossible. Who knows?"

The desire for children was a foreign concept to Tatum. She already had children. Five of them. Five fluffy, shedding children who had long outgrown the studio they all shared in downtown Detroit, just a short drive from Michigan Humane, where Tatum worked. "Like...*actual* children? You want real ones?"

Darla gave her a look.

Tatum raised her hands in defense. "Okay, *okay*. In the meantime, we've got a litter of puppies at the shelter.

They desperately need a foster placement. All our fosters are tied up with other litters." Tatum scratched behind Angus's ear. His left leg got going and his tail thumped happily against the laminate floor.

"I'd take a foster litter, *if* I had the space. *Or* the promise of a housing arrangement beyond May."

"What *are* you going to do?" In the week since Darla had called off her wedding, Tatum had given lots of thought to her sister's predicament. Not only was she losing her apartment, but so too was she losing an afford-able complex. "You could move in here, you know. Then you can stay near your job *and* save money. You'd be killing two stones with one bird."

Darla laughed and shook her head. "Two *birds*. One *stone*."

Tatum shrugged. "Whatever. You get my point."

"I love your *studio*, but Tate..."

Tatum nodded. "Yeah, yeah. I know. Plus, my kids would never stand for it." She winked at her sister, who groaned.

"Okay, back to my list."

"Right." Tatum resituated herself on the pull-out sofa. Angus leaped off and joined the others—one cat and three dogs—through the doggie door that spilled out onto a narrow cement balcony. Looking down at the list Darla had handed her, Tatum cleared her throat and again read from the top, starting over. "Number one: marriage." She glanced up at her sister, who sat up higher on the barstool, her self-pitying session apparently winding down. "Do you want me to put a check mark next to that or..."

Darla cocked her head, an unreadable expression darkening her features. "I mean, if I made an attempt, does that count?"

Tatum made a clicking sound with her tongue. "Nope. Unless you meant engagement instead of marriage."

"I do want a marriage," Darla confirmed wistfully, adding, "one day. A long, happy marriage."

"Number two," Tatum moved on, ignoring the fact that Darla had avoided her question. "Children. Shall I add that they can be furchildren?"

"Having dogs and cats is a given in my life. Just as soon as I have space for them. So that's a separate item, technically. I mean *human* children."

"Okay, okay," Tatum conceded. "So, we'll leave numbers one and two alone."

"They are the most time sensitive, however." Darla's face hardened, as if she dared Tatum to make an issue. "And as for the marriage one—*technically*—" She stopped midsentence. "Forget it. You're right. Let's move on."

Tatum cleared her throat and brought the page back up to her face. "Number three," she declared heartily before studying the short annotation thereafter. A smile flickered on her lips, and a question lifted her chest before she returned her stare to Darla. "Live on an *island*?"

2

"Haven't *you* wanted to live somewhere else?" Darla asked Tatum as they paused on number three.

Tatum didn't take long to ponder this question. "Of course I have. I want to live on a farm."

"A farm?"

"Yeah. A farm. In a little white clapboard house with a barn out back. Land for the kids, you know."

Darla smiled. "Right. The *kids*." She flicked a glance to the sunbathing crew on the balcony. They were a motley, hairy bunch. Tatum's whole world was out there on that balcony. When she looked back at Tatum, she was studying the list again.

She glanced up briefly. "Okay, marriage, kids, tropical locale, and then all these little things." Tatum read aloud numbers four through ten. "Scuba diving, white water rafting, learning to play an instrument, learning to quilt, learning a second language, staying in bed all day just for fun, working at an orchard." Tatum raised an eyebrow. "That's an interesting one."

"Which?" Darla asked.

"Well, the orchard." She squinted at the page. "And the staying in bed one. Haven't you ever been sick? That's the weirdest one, I'd say."

Darla giggled, then confessed, "I suppose it's less a bucket list and more a...a lofty to-do list or something."

"Bucket lists *are* to-do lists. Just big ones," Tatum offered. "And some people's are so far out there, they might as well be pipe dreams. Like mine, for example."

"*You* have a bucket list?" Darla smirked at her little sister. Tatum didn't seem to be the sort who needed a bucket list. When she wanted to do something, she just *did* it.

"Sure I do," Tatum replied. "But it's private."

Darla gave her a look then held her hands up in surrender. "Sorry."

"Don't worry about it. It's nothing scandalous. Just a... little thing. Like a promise."

"Oh." A million questions lined up behind Darla's one word. Silent predators to the otherwise Darla-centric conversation. Best not to go there. Not yet, at least.

One of the kids whined on the patio. Angus. He sometimes got skittish about crossing thresholds. Quirky guy.

Tatum stood and headed toward the patio door to usher him in, evidently thankful for the distraction. "They deserve more than this," she called over her shoulder, by way of changing the topic.

"I can't believe your landlord allows pets at all. We don't."

"Sunny View residents are different than downtown Detroit dwellers. Your tenants are college kids. Not real people."

Darla choked out a laugh. "I don't know what that has to do with a pet policy, but okay…"

"Anyway"—Tatum waved the topic off—"another thing I want to do, which isn't on any list, in fact, is to have *land*. *Space*." She drew her arms out in suggestion. "One day, I really do need to move."

"Out of this studio?" Darla asked. "Or out of Detroit?"

"Like I said. I'd love to be on a farm," Tatum proposed. "I really would."

"It's quite a jump," Darla pointed out, undermining her earlier implication that Tatum's dreams were too limited. Too small. "Studio to sprawling acreage."

"So is your island idea." Tatum lifted a knowing eyebrow.

"True," Darla admitted. She smiled at her sister. "True. But everything else is totally doable. I mean, I could go scuba diving tomorrow, if I wanted."

"You could also go to an island tomorrow, come to think of it."

"If you're thinking of my honeymoon plans, you're wrong. I gave the trip to Hunter." Darla pursed her lips. "Sort of like a consolation prize."

"Actually, no. We know of a place a lot closer than the Caribbean."

"What, Nantucket? I doubt that's within my budget."

"Think smaller. *Closer*," Tatum egged her on.

Darla rounded her lips into an O. "Mackinaw isn't exactly what I had in mind."

"Even smaller. Even *closer*."

Then, the lightbulb went off. Darla shook her head slowly at first, then quickly, pushing up from the bar. It was time to go. Tatum had officially lost her mind. "No way."

Her sister rose, too, letting the bucket list page—a page that wasn't easy to rip free from her planner—float to the floor. "Don't be stubborn, Darla."

She wasn't being stubborn. She was being realistic. "I'm not living there. Not with her."

"But you spoke. On the phone. Last week."

"Only because she called after you told her about Hunter." Darla squeezed her eyes shut. When she opened them again, the room was spinning. Focusing on Tatum became too hard. She found her way to the arm of the sofa and perched on it, gripping her knees.

Tatum joined her. "I know. She *wanted* to. She wanted to fix things between us."

"Us?" Darla rubbed her eyes. "You and Cadence seem just fine."

"I'm being delicate, Darla."

Shaking her head, Darla tried to clear her vision. The dizziness throbbed into a dull headache. "Can I get a water?"

Tatum moved to the kitchen and returned with a tepid glass. "Hey, this is *your* idea." She tapped the page she'd recovered from the linoleum. "*Live on an island*." Tatum bent and grabbed Darla's knees mid-drink. "You tried the marriage thing. The kid thing, too, I presume."

Ha. Darla rolled her eyes. "Don't go there."

"Well, why not skip to lucky number three?"

"Cadence wouldn't even *let* me live with her." Darla meant it as a dare, and Tatum clearly knew this.

Tatum's brown eyes flashed. "Oh, yes. She will. She'll let us *both* live with her."

3

It was a fib. Tatum had fibbed. Who *knew* if Cadence would let them ferry across Lake Huron and onto her deck? Not Tatum.

Even so, it was the only way to convince Darla to go. And Tatum *needed* Darla to go. She couldn't do this alone. She couldn't keep living in a studio with her furchildren and pretending that it was good enough for them.

It wasn't. But ever since Dad died...ever since he'd gotten sick, Mom, Tatum, and Darla had thrown everything they had into funding his end-of-life care.

It was time for Cadence to do her part now.

Tatum had to decide if she was going to call her eldest sister or...just show up. The shock of a surprise appearance by both Tatum and Darla could throw Cadence into a heart attack, sure. Then again, it could jump-start her heart. And, it could soften Darla's, too.

The next day, after she'd assured Darla she'd handle everything, Tatum did just that.

She handled everything.

"Hi," she said into the phone receiver. She'd gotten hold of the Birch Harbor marina. From there, they'd take the *Birch Bell* across the lake. If they wanted to bring their cars, that'd take some other wrangling, and Tatum wasn't up to such a task. She was, however, up to the task of planning the car ride to Birch Harbor and the ferry trip to the island.

Although, to be fair, Tatum could hardly see herself barging onto the island with five animals and a dazed, newly single sister. But, by the time she'd committed to her plan, it was even harder to imagine them both *staying* in Detroit. "I'd like to see about purchasing a summer package? I see on your website you offer long-term parking and ferry tickets?"

The woman on the line confirmed and provided prices.

"Great. Before I book, do you allow pets on the boat?"

Another confirmation. Tatum stored this information for the future, however. She wouldn't take them now. They'd stay with her mom. At least, initially.

After spending the last of her most recent paycheck in one fell swoop, Tatum took to her next task: requesting a sabbatical from Michigan Humane.

"We don't grant sabbaticals," her manager told Tatum.

Tatum balked. "Okay, then I'll need two months' leave beginning in May. Possibly three months. Depending."

"Tatum," the woman reasoned, "this isn't a tenure-track position. We can't save a part-time position for you. Not if you're going to be gone the whole summer."

A sigh filled Tatum's chest, but she forced it back

down. "I see. Well, Marsha, in that case, and I hate to do this, but I quit."

It was freeing. To quit like that. Tatum had worked at the shelter for ten years. She'd been paid just above minimum wage for ten years. Always hovering above that paltry baseline. The bare minimum. Never getting forty hours. Only ever thirty. Never getting benefits. Always forced to find another way. It wasn't the shelter she blamed, naturally. It was the system.

Still, Tatum alone couldn't change the system. Not yet, at least. Not while she was living in a studio with a balcony and five pets.

To change the world, Tatum knew she first had to change her own life. And anyway, who said Michigan Humane was the only place in the state to help animals? There were other shelters. And, where there weren't, there ought to be.

Maybe Heirloom Island needed that sort of thing, in truth.

Tatum picked up the phone once more.

Her recipient answered immediately. "Heirloom Island Animal Hospital, how may I help you?"

"Hi," Tatum began, smirking to herself, "I'm calling to ask, where is the nearest animal shelter?"

"If you're looking to surrender a—"

"Oh, no. I'm looking for a job. A job with a local shelter."

"Ah," the woman replied. "We don't have a shelter on the island. Neither does Birch Harbor. I know Tawas does, but that's a bit of a drive. And I could be mistaken, anyway."

"So, nothing local, then?"

"Nothing. That's why I was going to tell you, if you're looking to surrender, we can hold animals for up to forty-eight hours then transfer them to the county animal control. We do have some foster families around the island and some on the harbor but..."

Tatum thanked her and got off the phone. It was just a start. Just a little research call. Surely, she could find something on the island in the span of a couple months. That's all she needed to make her move.

Well, that, and a willing accomplice.

Darla did not know what Tatum's long-range plan was. All she'd agreed to was one summer. One summer sabbatical from her gig at the college. One summer away.

One summer with all three of the Sageberrys—or, as her mother dubbed them when they were little girls, the Sage Berries. One summer on an island, together.

One summer to fix the past.

4

Cadence emerged from her bedroom fresh for the day. Dressed in a simple black sundress—if sundresses could be black—she padded barefoot down the stairs and out onto the deck.

This was not the life she'd ever imagined. As the daughters of a factory worker and his hairdresser wife, Cadence and her sisters had grown up modestly.

For Cadence, the lifestyle didn't change once she graduated—barely—from college and entered the classroom. Private school teachers weren't necessarily better paid than public, at least not on tiny island towns in quiet Catholic schools.

But things had eventually changed for Cadence. Not least of which were her finances.

Presently, she lowered onto a chaise longue and watched boaters rip across the water, sending waves crashing to the shoreline. The water crept toward the boardwalk but never got nearer than that. Not really.

A glance to her right revealed Cadence wasn't alone.

Her stepdaughters were rummaging noisily on their deck, arguing over something, it sounded like. The stress of moving. And here Cadence was, sitting idly and listening in.

But she'd offered to help with the final boxes, and they'd declined. Three times over, she'd offered, and they'd declined.

They had no intention to shuffle furniture, especially with the very first vacationers arriving that night. They'd advertised the place as a furnished, long-term vacation rental. No sense in making more work. So, the girls would be over soon, locking the front door and trudging back to the place where they grew up in just a matter of hours.

Yes, Cadence lived next door to her stepdaughters. And down past their boardwalk house were other boardwalk houses that also belonged to the Van Dam family estate. Beyond the girls' place, there was one more. That last one the family treated as income property, renting it out as a vacation home or event venue. Cadence had taken on the duty of managing the property, and she still couldn't tell if Hendrik's daughters silently appreciated her willingness to do this or if they resented it.

Regardless, it was rented now, to newlyweds. An over-the-hill couple who'd eloped just the weekend before.

So, even when his daughters played coy, Cadence had other neighbors, too. Maybe even nicer ones.

The young women's conversation soaked the air and floated on a warm breeze to Cadence. Trifles of a life they'd soon be parting with. The freedom and independence that usually came with the early twenties. The sort they'd only brushed lips with, having stuck together, for one, and never quite grown up, for two.

Cadence wasn't sure where she or Hendrik or his first wife—God rest her soul—had gone wrong with the girls. Was it that they hadn't taken on part-time jobs as teenagers? Was it the money? Or, rather, the pretense of money?

Unusually anxious, Cadence slid lower on her chair, hoping that she could just relax and not worry about what the future held between her and her stepdaughters. Of what the future held for *them*, in particular.

A deep chime stirred her from what was to be a late-morning catnap in the warming part of the day.

The doorbell.

Frowning, she heaved herself into a sitting position and paused, waiting for a second chime—a confirmation that she, Cadence the Lonely Widow of Heirloom Island, in fact *did* have a visitor.

Soon enough, it came. The second knell.

She pushed up from the chaise, retied her kimono sash, and half jogged in through the house, the balls of her bare feet carrying over the cypress wood floor like a gazelle. Cadence was no gazelle, but she'd mastered the art of drifting quickly across her house. Most recently to make her way from the kitchen back to Hendrik, in the master, when he, too, rang his little bedside bell. Like a mad maid, she dashed, quiet as a mouse and quick as a fox. Her boxy body wasn't untoned, but those jaunts helped stave off extra pounds.

In the past several months, she'd kept them off, too. Her lack of appetite surely helped in that regard.

"Hello!" The air swept her hair off her shoulders as Cadence opened the door, greeting whoever was there before even seeing them.

"Hi" came a tentative, meek voice. A touch of Southern twang. Wholly familiar and strange all at once.

"Oh, *hi*." Cadence smoothed her silken robe down her torso, clenching her gut. "Liesel, right?" She flicked a glance to the man who stood off behind the woman. "And...Mitch?"

"Mark," the woman corrected bashfully, her lips curling around his name. One would never take her for a newlywed. Not at her age. At least forty-five. Possibly north of fifty. Even at either of those ages, though, the sandy-haired woman seemed so much older than Cadence felt.

"Mark," she echoed. "Right. I'm sorry." She glanced her fingers off her forehead as if to say *silly ol' me*. "How are you finding the rental?"

"Oh, it's *lovely*," Liesel gushed. "We were wondering about the ferry. It's hard to get the times from the internet, and we don't want to head down there only to wait."

"You're not...leaving?" Cadence asked. They'd only arrived the day before. Or was it two days before? Time was a fickle mistress on Heirloom Island. At least, for Cadence it was. The fallout from becoming a widow was her inability to track the days. Island time factored in, too.

"Well, yes," Liesel answered. "Just for the day. Is that... that's all right, isn't it?" She laughed nervously.

Cadence shook her head, embarrassed. She smiled.

"Oh, of *course*! I'm—I get confused easily. A side effect of living on the boardwalk."

Liesel and Mark stood awkwardly, waiting for her to do her job. Of course, vacation itineraries and day trips weren't exactly part of her job. She was simply the caretaker and property manager. Nothing more. Nothing less, however. The girls had tried to convince Cadence to keep Wi-Fi on at the rental, but she'd declined, opting to offer something of an off-grid vacation experience. Inevitably, this resulted in guests knocking on her door at all hours, thrown off by the fact that they had no cell service, no internet, and no way to enjoy themselves without either.

Only recently had she realized a brochure would be a professional thing to keep on hand. Even better, she ought to leave them in the rental before each new guest checked in. She made a mental note for next time.

Clearing her throat, she leaned back and plucked a folder from her foyer table. "I always forget. I meant to put this in your rental. It's got a brochure for the ferry, complete with times. You can also learn about the island, dining options, entertainment, so forth."

She passed it over and Liesel thanked her before asking, "I heard there's a nightly event on the boardwalk, near the dock? A soiree or a barbecue or something?"

"The Boardwalk Ball." Cadence felt a pang at even mentioning it. "It's not nightly. Weekly. But they don't do that anymore." She blinked through the omitted information.

Liesel raised her eyebrows. "Are there any local summer events?"

Cadence pressed her lips together, a visual apology. "So sorry, not until June."

Nodding, the couple again thanked Cadence and saw themselves off. Probably to the ferry. Definitely not to the Heirloom Boardwalk, a strip of island over which Cadence reigned queen.

Cadence and no one else. Not vacationers. Not the town. Not even the Van Dam girls.

She turned from the door to reattempt that nap, but just as she did, the doorbell chimed again.

5
_____

"Let me explain." Tatum held up both hands in surrender as Cadence stared, mouth agape, first at her, then at Darla.

Oh, Darla. Who slumped behind Tatum, her luggage hiked up to her underarms like an adolescent camper. Tatum mouthed an apology to her and turned again to Cadence.

"I know. You weren't exactly expecting us—"

"Weren't *expecting* us?" Darla fumed behind her. Tatum could sense her humiliation and ire, but here they were. One long car ride, one rocking, windy ferry ride, and then a brief cab ride from the Heirloom Island dock to the very edge of the boardwalk. The last house along Continental Coast. Cadence's house.

Tatum already missed the animals. She'd left them with Pat, their mom. Pat was a good animal-watcher, but she was no dog lover. This made Tatum antsy to get home. A touch regretful that she'd booked Darla and herself on a vacation to their sister's house...without first telling said sister.

Cadence finally found a string of words. "*Girls.*" She had always called them girls, Darla and Tatum. An affectionate collective nickname, and it felt even more affectionate, now that they weren't really girls anymore. "Come in. Please, come. Come." Following that came a broad smile and a darting gesture into the sand-swept house, all washed-out wood and nautical décor. Seashell imprints for art and anchors for doorstops. The woman had taste. There was no arguing that.

"Wow." Tatum took in the space. "Did you remodel? This place looks different than I remember. From the wedding."

All of the immediate Sageberry brood had attended Cadence's wedding, years back. Tatum and Darla, Mom, and even Dad. He was still alive then. Alive and unhappy about the nuptials of his eldest daughter to a man twenty years her senior. A man who was, well, nearly Dad's own age.

After the lakefront ceremony on the sand, the guests enjoyed hors d'oeuvres and cocktails across the three Van Dam properties. *Floating party*, Hendrik had whispered with a smirk to his new sisters-in-law. *Happens every weekend.*

Tatum was intrigued. So intrigued that she'd convinced Darla to explore with her. They moved in and out of each of the boardwalk houses, impressed and uncomfortable to take part in such apparent *wealth*. Odd wealth, too. Eccentric, old wealth of the sort that belongs to those families who carried generational traditions. And, maybe, secrets.

Back then, they'd been assigned to sleep in the house that was now rented out to vacationers. Meanwhile, the newlyweds and Hendrik's daughters had stayed in the main house. Hendrik's other family and a few close friends took the middle house, where the girls were now living.

Cadence moved them to the great room. "It is different. After Hendrik's passing, things have, well, changed." Her tone rang ominously, but Tatum chose to ignore it and review their adventure to the island.

She dropped her bags on a leopard-print rug and stretched. "There are no rideshares here. We were in a real, old-fashioned taxicab," she announced, by way of small talk.

"Heirloom is old school," Cadence answered, her voice softening and settling. She strode toward the back of the house—the kitchen. "What can I get you two to drink? Eat? You must be famished after such a trip. I recall the *Bell* doesn't offer much in the way of sustenance. Too short a ride."

"Ooh," Tatum replied, "I'd love a martini. And... cheese? Crackers? Whatever you fancy island people have on hand works for me." She beamed and fell into a cream-colored leather sofa with a *woosh*, stretching her legs out and her arms back behind her head like she owned the place. She sort of did. That was the thing about having sisters. *What's yours is mine.*

Darla threw Tatum a scathing glance then gave Cadence a short nod. "Whatever you have is fine." She joined Tatum on the sofa. "What were you *thinking*? You lied to me. You said we had an open invitation, but she had no idea! Seriously, Tatum?" Darla massaged her temples. "Ugh, this is *so* you." Then, her hands flew up and fell to her lap. "I don't even have an apartment to return to." She was reeling.

Tatum leaned forward and gripped the back of her sister's neck. "Darla, calm down. Cadence is our *sister*. We can stay here however long we want."

"Actually..." Cadence reappeared, a chic silver serving tray clutched in her hands, her lips pressed into a tight line. "I wish you could."

6

After leaving the tray with Darla and Tatum, Cadence retreated to the kitchen. Her cutting reply hung heavily in the air. Darla watched her go, and something burned through her core. Betrayal? No. It was anxiety. But not anxiety for herself.

Darla slid her gaze to Tatum, who'd begun helping herself to Ritz crackers and slices of American cheese. "Not exactly what I had in mind," Tatum complained through a mouthful.

Amazed at her little sister's denseness, Darla lowered her voice. "She just said we couldn't stay. And all you care about is the food?" She raised a hand toward the kitchen, glancing briefly to ascertain that Cadence was rummaging deep in the fridge, somehow unaware that she was the focus of urgent gossip. Not even gossip. *News.*

Tatum swallowed and rubbed her hands along her white jeans. The realization must have just struck her because a wild expression filled her eyes. She stood.

"Cadence," she called toward the kitchen, "what do you mean?"

Darla winced. She could have guessed that this would be the youngest Sageberry's response. Tatum didn't shy away from conflict. She welcomed it. Searched for it. Tatum was the sort to tackle her problems head-on, not beat around the bush. Not wait until the problem swelled into something unmanageable.

Unlike Darla.

She rose, too, and followed Tatum to join Cadence in the kitchen.

Cadence turned from the fridge, an unopened bottle of store-bought lemonade in her hand. Her face was white. White like her house, with its white-washed wood and pale oak floors and cream-colored sofa. Its seashell paintings and sun-bleached knickknacks. "Sorry," she whispered, setting the jug down silently and sweeping her thumb beneath each eye.

Darla stilled herself. There was too much wrong with the picture.

They were supposed to be on vacation, firstly. Maybe work through some past hurts with Cadence. Fine. Largely, though, they were supposed to be spending sunny days together on the deck with bottles of bubbly drinks and plates of fancy fruit. Like during the Van Dam-Sageberry wedding.

Now, Cadence was handwashing a glass in which to pour the lemonade, her eyes swollen from...what? Had she been crying before they came? Was she tired? Out of Botox rewards points? And then there was Tatum, tearing open a fresh bag of tortilla chips. Another one sat on the far side of the kitchen counter. Along with it, a set of paperware and plastic cups. Nothing made sense. Alternate reality. That's what Darla was in.

An itch crawled up her back and into her neck. She wanted to go. To leave.

"If I had any idea that Tatum hadn't made plans with you, Cadence, I would never have come. I'm so sorry. Whatever"—she held her hand palm up, limp—"whatever is going on in your life, I'm sure you want us to butt out. We'll leave."

At that, Cadence's head snapped up. "*Butt out*? You think I want to be alone? Why, because of what happened with Dad? You think I didn't want to be with you?"

Darla's hands fell to the tops of her thighs, and she worked her fingers into knots. "Oh, no. Cadence, I'm not bringing up the past. I'm just—"

"Oh, come on. Why can't we stay, Cadence?" Tatum plucked an overripe apple from the basket in the center of the island and took a deep bite, speaking as she chewed.

Cadence's eyes fluttered, and Darla saw she was bare faced. Not even a spec of mascara. A dab of blush. Nothing. And yet, she still looked...*good*. Then again, thirty-seven wasn't old. Cadence only *seemed* old because she'd married an old guy. Or an old*er* guy. And then he died. And he even died pretty young, but that he died made him seem even *way* older.

Darla untwisted her fingers and leaned against the island, accepting a glass of lemonade from Cadence's shaky hands.

The eldest Sageberry, who wasn't technically a Sageberry anymore, answered at last, her gaze on the window to her left. She looked through it, fixing her stare on the lake beyond. "The girls are moving back home." She blinked and returned her eyes to Darla and Tatum, pursing her lips primly. "Today."

7

Tatum froze at Cadence's admission.

"What do you mean?"

The girls were moving back home? What girls? And to what home? And what did that have to do with Tatum and Darla springing a summer visit on their sister? She exchanged a look with Darla. Darla's face scrunched in confusion, too. Or was it concern? "Oh!" A realization dawned on Tatum. "You mean the *girls*." Cadence's stepdaughters. For the past ten years, Cadence had considered Fay, Lotte, and Mila her own children. She'd never referred to them as stepchildren, either. Only real ones. Sort of like how Tatum mainly referred to her pets as her children.

Recently, however, the *girls* had forsaken Cadence's love. That was as much as Tatum knew. The details were in the devil. Or however it went. If such a saying even applied. She blew a wisp of her dark hair from her eyes and took another gulp of lemonade, eyeing Cadence as she drank.

"Right. Hendrik's medical bills chewed up his trust. We've got the properties. But family money..." Cadence fluttered her fingers into the air.

Darla finished her sentence. "Dust in the wind." Her tone was flat. Too flat.

Tatum set her glass down. She knew where this could go. Where Darla might take it. Her job was to steer the conversation away. Not fan the flame. "The Van Dams own Heirloom Island. No way are you or the girls destitute."

"No one *owns* Heirloom. She's her own island. We're just moments in time." Cadence was looking again through the window to the choppy waters beyond.

Tatum wasn't sure she understood. "But the Van Dams literally own the island. Didn't they, like, settle it?"

"The Bankses were the first family to settle Heirloom. Then came the Van Holts. Then the Van Dams."

Darla entered the conversation, though she seemed reluctant. "Tatum's right. The Van Dams have a heavy stake. But still, Cadence, how can you possibly be destitute? With all that old money. Family money." She gave Cadence a hard look, and Tatum squirmed on her barstool.

"Hendrik's ancestors settled the western coast *only*. And yes, this strip of real estate belongs to him. To his estate. But that's not much when you weigh it against everywhere else here. Every other residence. Every other business. Sure, the Van Dams are an old family. But that doesn't count for much anymore."

"It counts for three houses. Why do his daughters

need to give up theirs and bunk up with you?" Darla asked point-blank. "You've got the vacation rental."

"It's not enough." Cadence frowned. "You don't understand. His disease wiped us clean. We were at risk of losing all three houses toward the end. Thank God it didn't come to that."

Darla leveled her chin and slid her gaze to Tatum, who continued to squirm. "Thank *God*," she answered.

The tensions were crawling to a boiling point that Tatum had expected to come after a week, at least. Not a mere hour. She slapped a hand on the counter. "What's the going rate of vacation rentals on the island? Maybe Darla and I can float a few days in an Airbnb. Save the trip!" She said it with a cheer and pumped her fist.

Darla shook her head, her lips drawing down. "I'm not getting vacation pay for being here, Tatum. And neither are you." She looked at Cadence. "We shouldn't have come. Is there an afternoon ferry back to Birch Harbor? Maybe we can catch it."

Cadence's glare turned to ice. "The ferry runs every two hours. If you left now, you'd catch the very next one." Her face remained frigid and unmoving and her jaw seemed to lock into place.

Tatum's stomach started to ache. "Okay, *whoa*. Whoa," she inserted herself, inhaling deeply. "This place is huge. How many rooms you got? Maybe we can stay here and help. I mean, Cadence, won't it be *awkward* with the girls here? You'll need a buffer." Tatum wiggled her eyebrows at Cadence, whose face softened.

"A buffer?"

Darla added, "I'm not chaperoning a stepparent-stepdaughter reunion. Especially if things between you and them have gone bad."

"Who says things have gone bad?" Cadence answered, defensive. "It's just...we're under construction. We're grieving."

"Hendrik died almost a year ago. I get it if his own daughters are still grieving," Darla shot back. "But come on—" Darla appeared to change her mind. She shook her head, folded her arms over her chest, and looked at Tatum. "Never mind."

"Regardless, we'll make a party of it. I've always wanted to be a big sister," Tatum said. "Here's my chance. Or aunt. I'll settle for aunt. I can play aunt for a summer."

"A *summer*?" Cadence's eyes bulged.

Tatum shrank as both Cadence and Darla narrowed their gazes on her.

She held her hands up in defense. "I'm sorry—it's just —I didn't mean to make you both angrier. I just wanted a great summer. A fresh start, maybe. Maybe something new. For all of us. Right? I don't mind you both being mad at me as long as you *stop* being mad at each other!" Her voice rose up into a shriek.

The other two did not reply. Their stares remained on Tatum. Searing, cold stares the likes of which only sisters can effectively achieve.

Tatum went on. "Okay, what's that saying? 'The friend of my enemy is my enemy'?"

Her sisters exchanged a look, and like *that* the tension snapped. Shoulders fell. Weight shifted back. Heat lifted from the kitchen island and all three of them broke into laughter.

"You're terrible with idioms," Darla pointed out at last.

"I didn't go to college. So sue me." She shrugged, thankful for the break.

Still, it wasn't enough.

Worry settled deep in Tatum's heart. Deeper than she'd let on.

Because Tatum couldn't go back to Detroit. She couldn't go back to a studio apartment. She couldn't go back to the city.

Not if she was going to make things better for her kids and herself.

"How many rooms upstairs? How many down?" she asked once the laughter had died off and that awkward in-between silence fell over them like a shadow.

Cadence shook her head absently. "Um...three bedrooms upstairs. One down, but it's technically a parlor. We converted it by adding a wardrobe. My room is one of the three up. Each of the girls expects to move into her old bedroom, too." Cadence crossed her arms. "I want you to be here," she said as she looked at Tatum. After too long a moment, she turned her head to Darla, too. "I do. But—it's impossible. The girls' things are already here. I have no choice. They're upset as it is. Upset about moving home. To find you two here will make it worse. It will." She squeezed her eyes shut and rubbed her temples. "I'm sorry."

8

The logical thing was to drive her sisters back to the ferry. But this was also the cruel thing. Regardless of their poor planning and bad timing, she couldn't just shoo them away.

Were Cadence's hands *really* tied?

As Darla and Tatum each used separate restrooms to freshen up, Cadence set about putting together more than stale crackers and limp cheese. She'd make them lunch. They'd walk the boardwalk together. Chat. Make the most of things. Then, they'd stay for a night, and come morning, things would be clearer.

But even as Cadence whipped together an egg salad, guilt clouded her mind. What sort of awful sister kicked her own family out and ushered in other women? Sure, the girls were family. Cadence had tried everything in her power to make them feel like family, down to inviting them home once it was clear that they'd need to rent out their house, at least temporarily, until the eldest, Lotte, earned more consistent income.

Cadence fretted about *that*, too. She hadn't pushed the girls hard enough. Set a strong example. She'd let them skate by on their dad's dime, watching them grow up to be little more than spoiled brats. It was Cadence's fault they were moving into her house and she didn't have room for her *own* sisters.

She inhaled and peered through the kitchen window.

The trio were due the next day. Cadence had cleaned the rooms, set them up, of course. She'd been excited. Excited to establish a new bond. Maybe she could break the ice all over again. Maybe things would go well for the Van Dam gals, as Hendrik had lovingly called his four girls.

Maybe not.

The plans were in motion, though. Come Saturday, a new set of vacationers were due at the middle house on the boardwalk—the girls' house. In fact, this group was connected to Liesel and Mark, the other guests. Other reunion relatives. The two parties planned to host a small reunion at the rentals, which was the other part of why Liesel and Mark had ventured to such a tiny town. Family business. Cadence had offered to host a little dinner along their stretch of the boardwalk for a small added fee. Win-win.

Darla appeared in the doorway to the kitchen. She smiled. "So, tell me about the girls. They're older now, right? Do they work on the island? I remember you saying Mila might want to become a teacher."

Tatum joined Darla and the two eased back onto their barstools.

Cadence smiled at the memory. Mila had become

more than her favorite student. She'd become a daughter to Cadence. She was the glue that adhered Cadence to the Van Dam family. She'd brought Hendrik and Cadence together. Sparked their romance, inadvertently.

"She's twenty-two and spends her time in Birch Harbor, mainly. At the marina with this boyfriend or that. She goes to school at Baker College. Wants to get her pre-reqs done before she really decides about teacher school."

"And the other two?" Darla asked. "Faith and...Lucy?"

Cadence wasn't offended Darla didn't remember their names. Now was not the time to stir things up. It was time to heal. "Fay and Lotte. The older two. Fay is twenty-three. She wants to be a writer. Spends all her waking hours working on her debut novel. I suspect she even dreams about it. Lotte is twenty-five. A singer in a local band. Heir up There. She eschewed schooling, but she works hard to find gigs around the island and mainland. Sometimes, she even goes as far as Detroit. I know they sound like a burden. They're not." Blinking, Cadence pushed two bowls of egg salad across the table and took her sisters' glasses to change them out for ice water.

"They don't sound like a burden," Tatum replied. "They sound fun."

"Maybe you'd get along," Darla pointed out. "You aren't much older than them."

"I'm thirty. I may as well be fifty."

At that, Cadence snorted. Darla joined her. "Oh, Tatie. You realize you sound a lot younger when you try to compare yourself like that."

Tatum shrugged. "I'm just saying that to a girl who's

twenty-five, thirty sounds different. Older." She shook her head. "But anyway, I'd love to meet them again. It's been, what? Ten years? I can't even believe that."

"It wouldn't have been so long if—" Cadence bit back the words, regretting them instantly.

It was too late. Darla picked up where she left off. "If you had come home when Dad was dying."

9

U nwilling to meet with that particular topic of conversation, Darla apologized. "I'm sorry. That was unnecessary."

"One night." Cadence tied off the plastic bag of a baguette and pushed it down the island. "I'll drive you to the ferry tomorrow." She pressed her lips into a tight line and left.

Darla stole a glance at Tatum. "I shouldn't have done that."

"You really shouldn't have. We all know it was complicated. Why rehash?"

Darla replied, "How can she not regret it?"

"I'm positive she *does*, Darla. You badgering her won't make things better, you know."

Darla sucked in a deep breath. "I'm exhausted. Are we allowed to use the girls' beds?"

Tatum leaned back, looking for Cadence, probably. Darla stood, stretched, and strode for the sofas. "Forget it.

I'll crash here. Wake me up when everyone's in a good mood again."

As soon as her head hit the luxe cushions, Darla was out like a light.

Sometime later, she awoke groggily to the sounds of laughter nearby.

Long shadows stretched across the room, and for a moment, she forgot where she was.

Oh. Right. Cadence's house on the boardwalk. Heirloom Island.

Another thought crashed into her brain.

She had no apartment back home. Her job hung by a thread as the owner of Sunny View hired his daughter to cover things while Darla went to *figure her life out*. The owner's words. Not Darla's. Not even hippy Tatum's.

Darla rubbed sleep from her eyes and glanced around wildly for a clock. When she found none, she groped at her wristwatch and squinted through the darkened space. It was after seven. She'd slept the entire day away.

Just great.

Another cacophony of laughter spilled overhead, but Darla couldn't pin down the source. Bleary and confused, she pushed up, and a spell of dizziness hit her like a truck of bricks. She steadied herself on the edge of the sofa, waited a beat, then pushed up.

The dizziness fell away, and she managed to get her bearings.

The voices were now clearer, and Darla was fairly certain they were coming from the back of the house, the French doors that swept open onto a spacious deck that overlooked the Heirloom Boardwalk.

Still, once she neared the doors and crossed the bay window, slits of sinking sunlight cut into Darla's vision, and she couldn't tell if she was right.

She fumbled for the doorknob, and it rattled in her grip, taking her by surprise. Wasn't this Hendrik Van Dam's house? How could he have rattling doorknobs?

Before she could make sense of it, the door opened out, pulling her with it and spilling her onto the wooden deck and into the sunset.

"She's alive!" a voice sang out.

Darla squeezed her eyes shut. "What did you put in my drink?" She rubbed her head and focused on the face in front of her. Tatum.

"Cadence?" Tatum answered. "Did you drug this woman?"

Giggles erupted. Unfamiliar in their tone.

Darla squinted toward the rippling noise. Three other women, almost girls, actually, came into focus. "Oh," she murmured.

"Darla"—Cadence took her elbow—"you remember the girls? Mila, Fay, and Lotte."

"Hi!" returned a chorus.

Darla swallowed the remnants of her sleep. "Hi." She tried for a smile, studying each one. They were beautiful girls. Blonde and blue-eyed. Like Barbie dolls. Her smile grew. "I remember you three. You've grown up."

The one on the far right—Lotte?—laughed lightly. "Do you like burgers? We're having a homecoming cook-out. Sort of." Both bags of chips—the ones from the kitchen earlier—were propped open on a wooden table next to two lemonade bottles. All the paperware was set out along with condiments. Nothing fancy, but now it made sense. Darla rubbed her eyes.

"Our dad was the king of cookouts," one of the girls declared.

"I'm starving," Darla confirmed, her stomach rumbling. "So sorry to have slept the afternoon away. The trip really took it out of me."

"Are you feeling okay?" Tatum asked from her reclined position in a puffy cream chaise longue. A martini glass perched elegantly in one of her hands. Peeking out of the glass was a short stack of olives on a toothpick. Darla had been transported in time. Like she was back at the wedding, those ten years ago. The martini and the laughter. The smoky air—though there had been a much fancier barbecue back then, if she recalled. All of it was in stark contrast to the setting that had existed when Darla fell asleep.

She couldn't help but answer Tatum's question with a question. "What...*happened*?" she asked suspiciously. "I'm fine," she added, "but—"

"Well, Tatum bounced next door and dragged them over here, so I ran out and got burgers, and here we are!" Cadence beamed. Transformed from her earlier self, even.

"The guests are coming, too," the youngest girl, and smallest, added. Mila. This was the Van Dam daughter Darla knew best. The one who'd changed the course of history. The one on whom—if Darla was the grudge-holding type—she might lay blame to the fate of the Sageberry clan.

"Guests?" Darla sank onto the edge of Tatum's chaise.

"Liesel and Mark," Cadence answered. "Our honeymooners in Boardwalk House Number One."

"Boardwalk House Number One?" Darla was growing tired of being out of the loop.

"That's sort of how we refer to the properties. Number One, Two, and Three. Mine is Number Three."

"Ours, too, now," Mila chimed in.

"Hm." Darla nodded. "Oh, that's right. And you'll be renting out Number Two as of Saturday?"

"Hi up there!" came a cry from below. Someone calling up cheerily.

"There they are!" Cadence leaned against the wooden deck rail. "Come on up! Burgers are almost ready!"

10

Moments later, the deck was abuzz with life. A party had broken out, and Tatum couldn't quite pin down who was to blame. Was it her? For being the party girl that she naturally was?

Or Darla? For falling asleep and therefore permitting such chaos to take shape?

Or Cadence, for allowing all these veritable strangers to take over what could have, *should* have been a sisters' night in.

Once Darla came to and joined them, plates were dealt, buns tossed around, and burgers slid into place, and relative quiet descended against the backdrop of music one of the girls had set up. It floated out of a small round speaker propped on a side table.

"So," Tatum broke the silence after swallowing the last of her martini. "You two are on your honeymoon?" The question was for the distinctly out-of-place couple who'd meandered up from the sandy boardwalk below.

"That's right," the man said with a drawl. "Well, we

eloped. Got married at the Catholic church here. Turns out that's where Liesel was born, you see."

Tatum lifted an eyebrow to the quiet woman with sandy-colored hair. "You're from Heirloom Island?"

"No." She shook her head then crinkled her forehead, pausing. "Well, *yes*. I was born here, when the Catholic school was a school for wayward girls. Then I was put up for adoption. I grew up in Indiana. Near Louisville."

This amazed Tatum. Mainly because she didn't know Cadence's place of work had such a storied past. Also because it meant there was more to the story of Liesel and Mark's renting an entire house and Liesel's cousin renting a separate one. Some might assume it'd make more sense for family to split a rental the size of the boardwalk properties.

She couldn't help but poke. "St. Mary's?" The question was for either Liesel or Cadence, who still taught there, despite it all.

Cadence nodded. "That's right. A long time ago. Pregnant teenagers. Troubled girls, too. Now, though, it's just your average Catholic school. Small and modest."

Darla seemed to perk up a bit. "Do you have a drama program?"

Tatum leaned forward. She knew exactly where this was going, but it still caught her off guard.

"Drama program? I mean...we put on a Nativity play for Christmas every year. Sometimes the eighth grade will coordinate a production of Simon Peter."

Darla nodded casually then let it go.

But Tatum didn't. She pretended to explain Darla's question strictly for the girls' and the guests' benefit. *Not*

Cadence's. "Darla is an adjunct theater professor at Wayne State."

"Theater?" Lotte lit up. "That's cool."

Tatum glowed on Darla's behalf, but her sister shook it off. "It's fun, but it can get...tiresome."

"My cousin—one of the ones I was meeting this weekend—he's a choir teacher." Liesel pronounced choir like *quar*, and it took Tatum a minute to decipher. Then, another minute to piece together a triangulation between Darla, Lotte, and this mystery cousin.

She brightened. "Where? Maybe Cadence knows him if it's at St. Mary's."

"We don't have a choir teacher. We have Lotte." She dipped her head toward her eldest stepdaughter, who bowed.

"Thursday afternoons, assuming I don't have another gig scheduled." She smirked, and Tatum fell in friend love. She could see the Van Dam girls were a lot like her. Sort of...lost souls. Searching for a way to make life on their own terms. She didn't feel like Darla did—that they were spoiled. Obviously, they *were* spoiled, but Tatum could see there was more to the young trio than met the eye.

"How exciting," Tatum gushed. "To have *gigs*."

Mila broke in. "It's a rare occurrence."

Lotte elbowed her little sister, and Tatum empathized. Cracking jokes when you were the youngest set you up for retaliation. She smiled.

"Where does he teach?" Tatum asked Liesel.

"The high school there in Birch Harbor. He's from Heirloom Island originally, though."

"Really?" Lotte asked. "What's his name?"

Liesel hesitated a beat, proving that she really didn't know this cousin too well. "He's a relative on my birth father's side. I think he's removed a few degrees. The only way we got in touch was thanks to social media." Liesel hooked a thumb toward her new husband. "Mark here helped with that." They exchanged a knowing grin, and Tatum's gag reflex kicked in. She wasn't much for romance. "Anyway," Liesel rounded to her point. "His name is Mason?" It came out like a question. "Mason Acton?"

Mila gasped. "Mr. *Acton*?"

11

C adence bit her lower lip.

After leaving St. Mary's, Mila had had trouble at the high school. Spending two years on the island hadn't prepared her for a *real* school. Or, rather, had undone her previous public education. By the time she graduated from BHHS, she'd had a run-in with every last teacher there. But that wasn't how she knew Mason Acton.

Mila had observed him for one of her classes that very spring. The experience...didn't go well. In fact, it went *so* poorly that Mila had run home claiming she didn't want to be a teacher anymore. It was too hard. Teenagers were too cruel.

A taste of the girl's own medicine, some might say.

Cadence, however, considered it a lesson in perseverance.

She recalled telling Mila that just because students listened to the *real* teacher and not *her*, didn't mean much.

But they complained about me to him. While I was there! They said my mock lesson was boring!

Well, Cadence had shot back, *was it boring?* She pulled no punches. For Mila to fulfill her potential, it was good to observe and volunteer under the best of the best.

And according to all sources, that was Mason Acton.

Lotte smirked, well aware of their connection. "Mr. Acton is your cousin?" she asked Liesel.

Liesel shifted uneasily. "He's a distant relative. A link to other parts of the family I was set to meet this coming week."

Liesel perhaps didn't know how small towns worked, Cadence realized.

Then again, wasn't Liesel from some tiny little middle-of-nowhere farm town in Indiana?

Cadence tried to clear the air. "It's your family reunion. None of our business."

"Oh, well." Liesel grimaced. "Actually, I was meaning to talk about the whole reunion matter, Cadence."

"Oh?" Anxiety sprang to life in Cadence's chest. Everything was in place for the coming week. Liesel, Mark, and the Hannigan sisters would split the first rental. The Acton family would split the second. For a small added fee, Cadence and the girls would put on a beachy soiree, by way of a typical reunion meal. Something on the boardwalk that could spill down to the water. Something that would ignite the business venture for Cadence Van Dam. Save her from all the financial stress that hung heavily above her head since she'd cut that final check to the hospice service. "Is...everything okay?"

"The Actons had to cancel. I'm not sure why. Sounds complicated, but he was to split the rental with his mother and father, brothers. Cousins. Now they aren't coming."

"And what about the Hannigans?" Cadence asked. She knew the Hannigan sisters, newly arrived in Birch Harbor, spreading themselves out across the region like they owned the place. The Hannigan sisters were Liesel's relations, but Cadence couldn't quite recall how. The oldest three were set to share Liesel and Mark's rental. Based on other hints here and there, Cadence suspected money was a factor when they'd organized the trip.

"They're still coming. They don't—well—the problem is that there was a conflict, I guess. But the Actons won't make the reunion, sadly."

"But Mason Acton lives around here, right? How can he just... I mean, what I'm trying to say is that surely you'll bump into him." Cadence felt for Liesel. She understood, all too well, the pain of making plans to see family...then being forced to break such plans.

"Well, sure. I mean... Mason was mainly a vehicle to bring around that side of the family. It... It's a...long story. For another time. Mason was sort of the glue connecting us all, especially the Hannigan girls." Liesel swatted a hand. "Anyway, he and I can meet for lunch, I'm sure." She pressed her lips into a thin smile.

Mark appeared in the back door, a sheepish expression crossing his features. "'Scuse me, ladies. There's a gentleman in a boat out on your, uh, your dock down here. Says he's due here?" Mark dipped his chin toward Liesel. "I think he's here for the reunion."

12

D
arla watched with curiosity from just inside
the door. Her sisters rushed out with Liesel,
joining Mark on the back deck as the stranger
ascended.

Mila, Fay, and Lotte were bored with Liesel's drama—
or too interested in their social media lives to give a
bother. So, they slumped onto the sofa in a little line,
their faces aglow with phone screens.

The sight of them in the spot where she'd napped
reminded Darla that she and Tatum technically had no
sleeping accommodations for the night.

Stifling a yawn, Darla turned again to catch a glimpse
of the elusive reunion guest. Was it one of this Hannigan
clan?

Or had an errant Acton shown up after all?

Daylight had vanished entirely, but the dock was lit
well enough by porch lamps that Darla could be well and
duly taken aback to see the person of interest.

Not a Hannigan sister.

Possibly an Acton?

Maybe even this Mason Acton teacher character of Birch Harbor High School fame.

His strawberry-champagne hair picked up the porch light, burning like the head of a candle. She could even spy a charming smattering of freckles splashed across his face. Despite the reddish hair and freckles, though, he was all man. Tall and fit and tanned, even. Darla swallowed and took a tentative step over the threshold.

The others were fussing over him. Handshakes pumping, smiles exchanging. It was like a late-to-the-party guest who was supposed to be the main event. The spotlight on this ruddy, handsome stranger. A cross between Eddie Redmayne and Prince Harry. But a little older, it would appear in that warm deck light. A little...stronger.

Darla shook her head. Ridiculous.

"Oh! And *this*," Tatum gushed, as though Tatum had suddenly become the hostess, "is my older sister Darla."

Darla felt herself fall forward a step into their welcome ring. "Hi," she managed, suddenly aware of her sleep-crusted eyes and wayward hair. She patted at it and swiped a finger under each eye then gave a short wave.

But Mason Acton wouldn't have it. He pushed his hand through the circle of people, nearly brushing Darla's blue blouse with his fingertips. She blinked and accepted it, shaking and smiling as if she wasn't entirely arrested by his good looks and evident charm. "Darla."

"I'm Mason. Liesel's...distant relative, I guess."

"By marriage," Liesel corrected.

Darla caught something in her voice. A hitch. Like

there was a mistake. Then she remembered, and the memory fell out of her mouth like a pair of dice rolling down a craps table.

"Oh, the Actons. Right. They weren't coming, I thought?" She found herself locking eyes with Mason and quickly looked away. Her stomach churned like ripples across the lake, tickling her insides, thrilling her and nauseating her all at once.

To her immense relief, Mason laughed. His laughter was almost melodic, and she was reminded again that he, like her, was a teacher. But a choir teacher. Close to theater, sure. But also far. As far as here to the mainland, as everyone seemed to call Birch Harbor.

It was Cadence who broke the spell. "Mason didn't exactly get the memo," she explained.

He smirked. "I'm not on the best of terms with my father's side. The Actons can be a little chilly." He shrugged. "Anyway, it's a boat ride back home. No big deal."

"Oh," Cadence fretted, wringing her hands, "but you've paid the deposit. I'd hate for everything to just go to ruin."

"Could he stay with Liesel in the first house?" Tatum asked innocently, pointing down the boardwalk to the first house that belonged to the Van Dam estate, a white-washed wooden thing much like the one at which they now stood.

Liesel and Mark conferred semiprivately for a moment. "It'll be a full house there, as is. Mark and me in one room. Megan and her husband and daughter in another—which might be tight, anyway. Then there's

Kate and her partner and his daughter—and Kate's boys might make an appearance. That doesn't even include Amelia." She covered her face in her hands then reemerged miserably. "Oh, this is *so* awkward."

"You could spread out. Across the two houses? That could help?" Tatum was nothing if not a go-getter. Darla felt embarrassed for all parties involved and cut in.

"We don't know your dynamics here. Excuse my sister. She's an undying optimist."

"And you're a...what?" Mason cocked his head, and Darla felt as if it were just the two of them for a split second. "Pessimist?"

She balked then blinked. "I'm a realist. And a problem solver." Darla turned to Cadence. This was an easy problem to solve, actually. "He can take the middle house for one night. Tomorrow, you can host the soiree, and it's a win-win."

"We'll be here for a full week and half," Liesel pointed out. "We planned the party for Sunday."

Mason held his hands up. "Seriously, I really can hop in my boat and head home. Liesel has my number, so we can—"

"Wait a minute!" Tatum's face lit up and she snapped her fingers and wriggled her bejeweled fingers in the air excitedly. "We'll do a vacation share!"

"What's a vacation share?" Darla now knew better than to trust any off-the-cuff idea of Tatum's.

Cadence gave Darla a look, confirming her right to be wary.

Tatum proceeded with her idea, her excitement only growing. "We'll split the house. Cadence will give us a friends-and-family discount, and we can stay the week with you, Mace."

"It's Mason," Darla corrected through gritted teeth, silently seething and flushing and blushing and...totally intrigued now.

Tatum waved her off. "Yeah, I know." Her eyes shimmered. "One week. That house has two stories. We'll take the upstairs. You take the downstairs. We'll be over here all day, anyway. You'll never know we're sharing a house." She winked at him. "Whatdya say, *Mace*?"

"What about me?" Darla complained. What she wanted to remind her sister of was their paltry budget. They intended this vacation as a low-budget thing. Now they'd be responsible for splitting the cost of a three-bedroom house on the *boardwalk*?

"Okay, what do *you* say, Darla?" Tatum crossed her arms and cocked her head, ignoring Liesel and Mark, who continued to chew on their nails anxiously.

"I say," Cadence cut in, her jaw set and expression unreadable, "that it's a plan."

13

Tatum took it upon herself to explain everything to Mason and Liesel and Mark. Why she and Darla weren't staying at Cadence's house. Why Cadence's daughters were hunkering down there for now. So on and so forth. Sure, she probably overshared, but who cared?

It's not like they'd ever see these people again.

One summer.

Tatum kept reminding herself of this.

Now, she just needed to figure a way to fund one summer in that gorgeous house next door to her sister's. She had her eye on the prize, but if Cadence was serious about needing the extra cash, Tatum wasn't afraid of finding a summer gig.

Not one bit.

Now, she needed to turn her attention to the matter at hand. Hauling everything next door and getting acquainted with their new roomie, Mason.

Darla, who'd been acting weird ever since she woke

up from her nap, settled financial details with Cadence and Mason while Tatum coordinated the moving of their luggage. Mark, Liesel, and the girls helped, each carrying one piece through the front door and across the sandy walk some yards until they marched up a short stoop and in through the front door.

Tatum flipped on the lights and promptly let out a sigh.

Liesel and Mark bid her and the girls good-night and took their leave.

Tatum turned to the three sisters. "I'm sorry," she said glumly.

"Sorry for what?" Lotte answered, folding her arms over her chest. "It was never *really* ours, you know?"

"And we never *really* wanted it, anyway."

Tatum lifted an eyebrow. "Back up. You never wanted to own a house on an island on a *boardwalk*, free and clear? And one that looks like this?" She waved her arm across the brightly lit space. Like Cadence's, it was decorated in cool beachy blues and muted, natural beiges. Darker navy stripes cut across the rug and matching throw pillows. It could be a house from a catalogue. Designer digs. Tatum shook her head.

But Fay jumped in. "I've always wanted to live in the woods. Maybe even a mountain. Someplace where the snow gets trapped in the pine trees. Where the air smells like woodsmoke. Someplace dark and moody." She smiled a smirky sort of smile. "You know?"

Mila went next. "I want to live in the suburbs. With a husband and two kids and a green lawn out front. No lake where they could drown." A shadow crossed her face.

Tatum figured it was the emergence of Cadence, Darla, and Mason in the doorway behind them.

"And you?" Tatum asked Lotte. "Let me guess. Europe?"

"Nashville. I want to be a country singer." She sighed wistfully. "One day."

Cadence clued into the conversation right away. "The grass is always greener," she interjected, making way for Mason to stride through with a duffel slung over his shoulder.

"Is that why you moved to an island?" Tatum asked Cadence. "You wanted a change?"

Shrugging, Cadence pressed her hands together. "Girls, what say we put on Lifetime and veg on the sofa? I'm spent."

Tatum rolled her eyes. Ever the one to avoid conflict. To avoid hard choices. That was Cadence. Cadence, Darla, and Mason said good-night.

After locking the front door, Tatum turned to see that it was now just the three of them. Two exhausted, displaced sisters and one uncommonly upbeat, out-of-place stranger. In a house together. For an entire week.

Chewing on her lower lip, Tatum wondered if maybe, for the first time in her life, she had made a big mistake.

14

The next morning, Darla woke up feeling about the same as when she'd gone to bed. First and foremost, she was confused. The puffy white down comforter and seashell artwork. Washed-out wood floors and navy-and-white-striped rugs.

When she pushed up from the too-soft bed, a headache hit. Lack of caffeine first thing was surely to blame.

Lastly, came a spell of dizziness. Maybe this was to do with being on the water and staring out to see waves dip and bump across her window?

Regardless, she promised herself that she was not going to wallow. She was not going to complain.

Cadence had given them a steep discount to split the house with this Mason guy. She'd reasoned this quiet concession would make her other guests happy and keep Tatum and Darla in town for a bit. It was the best any one of them could hope for in an otherwise awkward situation.

Still, she wondered about Mason. If he really did have a house in Birch Harbor, why was he so quick to agree to stick around the island for a reunion where he'd be the odd man out?

And what was his family conflict that had set in motion his *missing the memo* on the Actons' bailing?

These were all questions Darla felt she'd better get to the bottom of. Especially, if she was going to share a house with this man for a week.

Then, once she'd ensured everything was in order, Darla could tackle the other reasons for which she'd agreed to come to Heirloom.

One, enjoy island life, of course.

And two, patch things up with Cadence.

Of all of her tasks, solving Mason Acton, achieving her bucket list dream of just *being* there, and fixing the past with her sister, it was the last one that proved the most complicated. The most daunting.

The most impossible.

"Morning!"

Darla was greeted by a cheery, freckle-faced breakfast chef.

Good thing she'd showered and got herself pulled together. Despite the earlier dizziness, she was feeling more like herself. Now, all she needed was a strong cup of coffee, and she might be able to confront the day after all.

"Morning." Her stomach did flips and flops all over

again. "Where did the groceries come from?" She studied the scene with a touch of awe. He had a crate of eggs propped open, half of the dozen sizzling in a skillet presently. The toaster was filled with four slices of what appeared to be wheat toast, Darla's preference. And the distinct and succulent smell of bacon filled the downstairs.

Not only that, but a fresh pot of coffee percolated on the countertop. And still, despite the movie-quality scene complete with a boyish hero, only the coffee sounded good to Darla.

She was too nervous to eat in front of this man.

"Your sister dropped off a couple of bags of stuff earlier," Mason replied, flipping the spatula like a pro. "Take a seat. I'll have your plate ready in five."

"Oh," Darla responded, too unsettled to follow his directions. "Was it Tatum? Tatum who got groceries?"

"No. The leader." He smirked at her, flipped the spatula into his left hand, and—with his right—slid a plate down the bar and into Darla's slightly shaky grip.

She gave him a look. "The *leader*?"

"Yeah." Mason grinned and twirled the spatula again, sliding it beneath a panful of fluffy eggs and turning them onto a waiting platter. "She seems like she's the leader."

"That's only because she's the eldest." Darla poured coffee and twisted to the fridge, rummaging helplessly for creamer.

"Will whole milk do? I gather your leader takes her coffee like an alien, because she forgot the creamer." He hooked his finger into a nearly full jug of milk and handed it out to her, his other hand balancing the platter of scrambled eggs.

She accepted the jug and then he passed her an aluminum coffee thermos with the words *Don't Hassle Me, I'm Local* etched across in jagged scratches. A souvenir that had long outworn its sense of humor. Even so, Darla laughed. "Any other vessels?"

He cocked an eyebrow. "Vessels?"

She set the thermos down. "This is weird, but I prefer to drink out of..." She realized how ridiculous and picky she sounded as she eyed the steaming porcelain mug that sat at the far side of the stove. Mason's, no doubt.

He followed her gaze. "Oh, you mean like a normal mug? What *are* coffee mugs made out of, anyway?" He grinned, and Darla couldn't tell if it was his smile or his teasing that was more tantalizing to her.

"I see you found a normal mug." She propped her hands on her hips.

Mason flared his nostrils and shook his head. "I happen to prefer normal ones, too. And it would appear this vacation rental has the most hodgepodge collection of coffee mugs of any in which I've stayed."

A showdown. Not only that, but a diss to her sister. Darla wasn't going to take the bait. "Actually," she replied, "I like this one, anyway."

Mason shrugged, but the stitch of his lips told her he'd won, and he knew it. And it told her that he also knew they were flirting.

Darla felt ashamed and grabbed the silly thermos, rereading it aloud. "Don't hassle me. I'm local. Sounds like an islander thing."

Mason laughed. "Sure is. It's a tourist town thing. I haven't been in this area, but locals sure are funny about being, well, local." He lifted his chin in indication of her tumbler, which Darla studied again, like she could solve the world's problems if only she, too, could be a local. As though he read her mind, he added, "We should make a mug that says *Don't Hassle Me, I'm on Vacation.*"

"How about *Don't Hassle Me No Matter Where I Come From.*" The words took on a deeper meaning than she'd meant, and she sensed he could feel that, too.

"I like that," Mason answered. "*Just Leave Me the Heck Alone While I Figure Out My Life.*" He laughed, a half of a laugh. In that moment, Darla knew they shared more than just a boardwalk house for a week. She didn't know what. And she didn't know if Mason and she would ever arrive at a place where they might share their pasts...but it was *something*.

Darla gave him a nod. "Yeah. We should go down to that little one-stop shop at the dock in town and have them make one for us."

Mason grunted appreciatively through a sip of coffee. "Let's do it."

If only.

Darla poured her coffee and milk and changed the topic of conversation. "Thanks for doing all of this," she said, indicating the breakfast spread. "You really didn't have to."

"I wanted to," he answered. Without waiting for her reply, he whipped around to pop the bacon out and pressed the conversation ahead skillfully. "Tell me, what brings you to the lovely Heirloom Island? Are you ladies having a reunion, too?"

Ignoring the question briefly, Darla pointed to the toast. "Mind if I help?" She could stomach toast. It would calm her nerves. And if he was going to all this trouble, Darla knew she'd better at least pretend to have an appetite.

"Be my guest."

"And to answer your question, yes. Tatum and I are in town to visit Cadence. We, um, we didn't plan well. We just sort of showed up. That's Tatum for you. She's..."

"A wild card?"

"Impulsive." Darla sorted out the toast, pulling butter from the door of the fridge—leftover from the girls, no doubt—and jam from the pantry. "She means well."

"She reminds me of somebody's wacky aunt, except about twenty years too young."

At that, Darla burst out laughing. The description was perfect. Tatum was exactly a wacky aunt. Just...an aunt with no nieces or nephews. Then again, she did have the Van Dam girls.

Feeling emboldened to reveal a little more, she added her own jab. "And how exactly do *you* fit into your family puzzle? You seem hard to pin down yourself." She eyed him over her mug, blowing on it to cool the hot liquid.

He pretended to think then frowned and shook his head. "Seeing as I'm a little disconnected from them, I couldn't really say."

"Ah, because they forgot to tell you they were bailing on the family reunion." Which begged a whole other question. Darla considered pushing further, but she didn't need to.

"I'm not close to them. I only wormed my way here because I was looking for a vacation and happened to find myself in an email thread. They probably didn't know I was coming."

This only served to add a new question to Darla's inquisition. Why wasn't he close to his family?

But she knew better than to open *that* particular can of worms. She, herself, was in a similar predicament.

"You were looking for a vacation...in your own town?" she tried a different angle entirely.

He snickered. "Aren't staycations all the rage? Anyway, yeah. I'm helping organize Birch Harbor's Summer Stock in a couple of weeks. I can't go far."

"Summer Stock?" Darla's eyes grew wide. "That's a theater thing. Not a...high school choir thing."

"Not normally, no. But I like to chip in. I'm a single guy. My friends are all married with kids. Gotta find stuff to do." Then, he winked at her. *Winked*.

It felt like a critical moment in the progress of their roommate relationship. Darla searched for the right transition. A transition away from the wink. Into a similar line of convo, where she could extract more info without giving away too much of her own. "I, uh...I teach, too."

"Oh, you do?" He popped his thumb in his mouth, clearing away bacon grease or something, and Darla remembered that this guy, no matter how attractive, was a stranger. A total stranger who just happened to *sort* of share her profession. And that was it. And, *oh*, where on *earth* was Tatum?

Sleeping, of course. It was past nine, and she was sleeping.

"Yes," Darla confirmed, swept away by the clatter of forks and plates and their somehow synchronized movement to the bar together, settling at their plates, each with a steaming mug of coffee and a sweating glass of ice water. Like a pair of old friends, almost. "I'm an adjunct professor in the fine arts department at Wayne State."

"Ah, wow. *College.*"

"Right." She took a tentative bite of toast, her stomach settling immediately, even though she could feel crumbs collecting at the corners of her mouth. She covered the lower half of her face and reached for a paper towel. "Anyway. I'm not tenured, so who knows?" *Why* would she say that? Act like her future was up for grabs? It definitely wasn't. In one week, she'd be back in Detroit. Gearing up for another semester. Sure, originally, she'd planned not to return until late July, but what was the difference? She was absolutely, positively going back to the theater department. No, she hadn't signed her contract yet, but—

"So, which one do you teach?"

"Which what?" She swallowed her bite and took a slow sip of coffee.

"Which fine art?"

"Oh." She laughed lightly. "Right. Theater. Not what you think, though."

"Not what I think? What would I think?" He gobbled down his eggs like he hadn't eaten in a month.

"Well," Darla began, not wholly aware of just how comfortable this all was, "I teach stage management.

Most people hear *theater* and think *actress* or something." She shrugged. "I'm more behind the scenes."

Mason held her gaze, a slice of bacon stranded in midair between them. Her coffee cradled in both hands as she waited for his answer. He didn't lower his voice or soften it. He blinked then said, clear and sensuous as day, "Well, that's a dang shame."

15

"What's a shame?" Tatum asked as she rounded the kitchen bar and reached greedily for a mug and the coffee carafe. Pouring with one hand, she tugged the rubber band from the bottom of her black braid. She didn't always have the presence of mind to plait her hair before bed, but when she did, she could count on at least a modicum of volume and body the next day, rather than limp, lifeless locks of dark-colored straw. Was dark-colored straw even a thing?

She didn't think so.

Darla and Mason answered at once.

"Oh, nothing," Darla said quickly.

But Mason's answer came out different. "That your sister is a stage manager type and not a starlet type."

Tatum rubbed sleep from one eye and studied him. She was lost. "Mind if I grab a plate?"

"Help yourself," Mason answered through a mouthful.

Tatum liked Mason. He was comfortable. Normal.

He'd make for a good roommate. At least, as good a roommate as any, especially in this predicament. Tatum still wasn't sure where the week would go. How they'd get along with a strange man in a strange house on a strange island with a nearly *estranged* sister. But they would. In fact, they *had* to. That was the thing when you went on a vacation without making firm plans: you were beholden to the whims of the vacation. Mistake or not, she and Darla had officially entered survival mode. They had no choice but to make it work. "So," she went on. "I don't know about you two, but I'm going to seize the day."

"Oh, really?" Darla asked. "How?"

Tatum dipped her mug toward her sister. "I was going to ask you the same thing. You're the one whose bucket list we're doing."

Darla made a sort of choking sound.

Tatum set her coffee down, panic rising in her chest. Choking scared her. She went for her phone, ready to dial 9-1-1. "Are you okay?"

Mason gave Darla a solid clap on the back, and it served to make things better, Tatum was pretty sure.

Darla coughed and rubbed a paper towel across her face and, when she recovered, glared fully at Tatum.

"Oh my gosh. You scared me." She regained a regular breathing pattern and pressed a hand to her chest. "Slow down and chew your food, Darla."

Darla's glare returned, but she quickly wiped it away, taking a steady drink of water and clearing her throat at last. "Anyway," she said with false brightness, "I figure we could rent kayaks or go to lunch. You know. Normal vacation stuff." She laughed, and Tatum was fairly certain it was the nervous sort.

She studied her sister.

Having cleaned his plate, Mason interjected, "This is a bucket-list trip?"

At that, Darla laughed even louder. "Well, no! *Yes*. It's just, you know. I'm—I figure you're never too young to follow your dreams, right?"

Tatum watched in fascination as Darla covered her face in her hands. It all came together. Darla had a crush on Mason.

Did he return it? Should Tatum ask?

She knew better than that. Instead, she tried to help. "Exactly! That's why I'm here, anyway."

"You have a bucket list, too?" Mason scratched his head. "Maybe I need to get one. What do you put on a bucket list?"

"Well, mine just has the one item," Tatum said, trying her hardest to distract them from Darla's embarrassment, or whatever it was that kept her hiding behind her hands.

"What's that?"

"It's a secret," Tatum said proudly, a wide grin stretching over her face.

Mason narrowed his gaze suspiciously on her. "Huh."

Darla finally emerged. She propped an elbow on the table, leaned into it, and hooked a thumb toward Tatum as she faced Mason. "You're right."

The two exchanged a knowing look, and Mason answered as though Tatum wasn't in the room with them. "Wild card."

16

After dropping off groceries for Mason and her sisters, Cadence hurried home. They were closing in on the reunion, and even if it was to be attended by a smaller group, she knew she had to make it count.

Mila, Fay, and Lotte had agreed to help. They'd split the profits, after paying the monthly bills.

Cadence hadn't had to follow such a tight budget since before she married Hendrik. But at least she knew how. Now it was time to teach the girls.

They started with a shopping list and a planning list. Cadence wasn't great at planning, truth be told. She had poor organizational skills, preferring to fly by the seat of her pants and go with the flow.

Now, though, that wasn't an option. They needed a clear idea of what Sunday evening would look like. If this thing went well, it could be very good for the Van Dams, or what was left of them. It could position Cadence as *the* island event gal. Wedding? Go to Cadence Van Dam. Graduation party? Cadence on the Boardwalk, of course!

Returning to the classroom the coming year would help stabilize them, but if the girls stuck around without making good salaries, they would have to pool their resources even more than just sharing a house.

It was Mila who wandered into the kitchen first, pouring herself a glass of orange juice and settling at the kitchen island with her phone.

"What are we doing today?" she asked between drinks.

Cadence sighed contentedly, working on her own coffee. Suddenly, it was like old times again. She was the mom—or as close to it as she'd ever get. Mila was her favorite. Stepmoms were more prone to favorites than biological mothers, she was pretty sure.

"We need to plan the reunion, mainly. Maybe shop, too." She paused, thinking. "Do you think we need flowers? Balloons?"

Footsteps echoed along the wood beyond the kitchen. "No balloons!" This from Fay.

"Flowers depending," Lotte added. The two older girls helped themselves to coffee then joined their little sister.

Cadence was starting to wonder if this wasn't such a bad setup after all. Having the girls back could even be...therapeutic.

"Depending on what?" she asked Lotte.

"Our budget."

"And our budget," Fay went on, like she was a pro, "depends on what you're charging."

"What *are* we charging?" Mila asked helplessly.

Cadence gave them the number she'd relayed to Liesel.

Three jaws dropped.

"You're joking," Fay accused. "You figured you could cover costs on *that*?"

Cadence blanched. "I didn't want her to go elsewhere. You know there's that place in Birch Harbor. And at the time Liesel booked, it seemed like a huge party. Not a small group. Have I ruined everything?"

Mila shook her head. "We'll figure it out. Maybe we do some additions that are low or no cost?"

"Like what?" Cadence asked.

"I'll provide entertainment," Lotte volunteered selflessly. "I've got my sound equipment. The band. We'll set up and handle music and MC duties."

"I can write up the menus," Fay offered. "It's not much, but it'll make the party seem fancier."

"We just need someone to, like, *coordinate*," Mila pointed out.

"That's me," Cadence replied. "And you, too, Mimi," she said, using the girl's old pet name.

The three of them all glanced at one another before looking back at Cadence.

"What?" she asked, disquieted by their expressions.

"Cadence, we know you want to make money. And you're definitely...good at being in charge. But should you *really* coordinate?" Lotte pointed out.

It was a slight, and it landed as indelicately as it could have. Cadence balked. "Of course I should. This whole thing was my idea." She hated to sound so defensive. But who else was there to run the event? And why *shouldn't* she?

"Cadence," Fay said, her voice low, "don't you remember what happened last time?"

Squinting and shaking her head, Cadence finally answered, "No? What do you mean *last time*? I've never thrown a reunion party before."

It was Mila who lay her hand across the top of Cadence's. Gentle. Sweet. "Dad's funeral."

Feeling faint, Cadence simply replied, "Oh."

The first thing for Darla to do was rejoin Cadence.

Now that she was alone, she could do just that.

Mason planned to head up to the first house to visit with Liesel. He said he intended to make the most of the reunion thing.

Tatum had gone to town to grab a newspaper. This was an odd errand, in Darla's opinion. But then, Tatum was an odd person.

Alone, Darla crossed over sandy wooden planks to the third house on the boardwalk. A tad nervous to show up unexpectedly all over again, she knocked faintly.

The door opened within moments. "Oh, thank *goodness* you're here." Cadence didn't wait around. She waved Darla in urgently, smacking in her beige sandals across the house and toward the living room, where three blonde heads bobbed together in a huddle over the coffee table.

"Is everything okay?" Darla sensed everything was *not* okay, but then...when was the last time she'd been around Cadence in an emergency? Over ten years. Maybe fifteen. It could have been when they were kids—nearly two decades ago. Maybe Cadence had turned more panicky in all that time.

"We need someone like you," Cadence said, falling into one of two matching sitting chairs. She pointed for Darla to sit in the one opposite.

Darla did. "Like me?" Her dizzy feeling had returned in fits since that morning, spiking when Mason left and spiking again when she made the choice to come to Cadence's. If this was what generalized anxiety disorder felt like, she was ready for her Fluoxetine, please.

"You're a director, right? You direct plays," Cadence insisted.

Confused still, Darla shook her head. "No," she said slowly. "I mean...not *exactly*."

"Well, then what *do* you do? I thought you were in charge. You know, the theater queen who hovers above everybody with a clipboard and a beret." Cadence fiddled her fingers together.

"I teach stage management. The clipboard is the right idea, I guess, but—" Darla looked at the girls, who finally looked up. Three pieces of paper lined the coffee table in front of them. "What's this about?"

"This reunion party I'm putting on. I don't know the first thing about parties. I mean *seriously*, Dar." Cadence looked wan. Washed out and depleted. Tired.

She replied, "You're really stressed, aren't you?"

"Yes," Cadence swore. "*Really*."

This, for some reason, amused Darla. It shouldn't. It should worry her. It should move her to action. But she sort of liked drinking in the moment. The moment when her older, cooler, richer, more aloof sister—the one who had it all—*needed* something. Was *stressed*.

"You have three helpers here, though." Darla looked at the girls. "You're helping Cadence, right?" she asked them.

They each nodded, then Lotte held up a page. On it, a list. Darla studied it. Random ideas floated in neat columns. Drinks and food in one and *miscellaneous* in the other.

"This is a great start," Darla confirmed. "Seems like you've got it under control. Anyway, it's just a small reunion. No Actons, remember?" Using the common lingo—the guests' last name—made Darla feel invested. She liked that.

Lotte diverted the conversation. "Are you really in *theater*?" The way she asked this made it sound like Darla should be famous.

She leaned forward and pretended to reread the notes, like she had anything meaningful to contribute. "Yes, but not how you think. I teach at Wayne State."

"Have you...acted on Broadway or anything?"

At that, Darla couldn't help it; she laughed. Shaking her head, she replied, "Not exactly. I'm not an actress. But I have worked on Broadway, yes. A couple of small theaters. Small production companies. Small *everything*. You think of New York, of *Broadway* as this sweeping, glamorous place, home to celebrities and art heroes and heavy velvet curtains with adoring audiences and perfect lighting." Darla blinked. "It's not always that."

Lotte shifted back on the sofa, disappointed, perhaps?

"But you put productions on, right? That's what Cadence told us. That's why you could help with this, right?" Behind the thick black eyeliner and overmuch rouge and bronze, Lotte's face was inscrutable. Darla liked her. She was persistent. She'd need that in the entertainment biz. If she really did pursue it.

"Yes, I guess you could say that. I never produced anything, but I've done some assistant directing and lots of stage management. Lots of management in general. And, now, teaching." Darla didn't mind being in the spotlight for a little while. She indulged them—*and* herself. "A reunion party—or any party—is a lot like a play. The best parties have at least a small degree of rehearsal. It's what makes weddings such popular events." As she said it, her gut twinged again, and the dizziness throbbed back to life in her head. She squeezed her eyes shut.

Weddings.

"I always figured what made weddings popular was how expensive they are. And...I mean...it's, like, a *wedding*," Mila pointed out.

"Remember when Dad and Cadence got married?" Fay asked, a dreamlike quality in her voice.

Darla managed to steal a look at her sister, whose expression turned sad.

Setting her jaw, Darla wasn't wholly certain she had a place in this reflection, in this memory.

"Yeah," Mila answered. "That was the best day."

What? Best day? Mila really thought that her father

remarrying a younger woman—Mila's own teacher, in fact—was not only a good day, but the *best*? Darla stilled her judgment as well as she could.

"You remember, Darla?" Cadence prodded. "I thought Mom was going to float across the lake on champagne. It was like she'd never had it before! Dad, too."

Darla did remember, but her memory felt different. Muted. Like it existed in an alternate reality. A sad memory, not a happy one or a funny one. She rounded her mouth into the shape of an answer. Something kind. Something...true.

"It was a beautiful day," she managed.

And it was. The weather was Michigan-perfect. Not too hot. Not too cold. Not wet or overbright or humid. Darla had been to her fair share of miserable weddings. Shivering in a shawl. Sweating in an evening gown. Cadence's wasn't that.

Would Darla's have been?

Maybe she shouldn't help with the reunion. Maybe it'd dredge up all the crud she'd only just buried.

Maybe she should crawl back under the white down comforter and stare at a shadowbox of seashells and sand dollars until another nap stole her away, and she could wake back up and eat breakfast with Mason Acton again. And pretend that she wasn't staying next door to Cadence Sageberry-Van Dam.

The sister who moved away and never, ever looked back.

18

"Downtown" Heirloom Island was too cute, by Tatum's standards. Actually, by anyone's standards. It had all the vibes of a San Diego fish market coupled with that of Birch Harbor's touristy marina *plus* a Midwestern, down-home, small-town quaintness.

How did they do it?

Tatum decided to get a second breakfast from the Island Koken, an old lakefront house-turned-café. There, she found everything she needed: a *beschuit* with chocolate sprinkles, an outdoor table where she had a good view of local dog-walkers, and yesterday's paper, folded wonkily and coffee stained.

Stealing a crayon from the plastic tub next to a stack of children's menus, Tatum then settled in with her treat and the classifieds and set to work.

Within an hour, she'd scrawled out five leads on her napkin, devoured her food and a glass of juice, and left the dregs of her change purse for a tip. It amounted to over twenty percent, which pleased Tatum, even if it meant she was totally and officially out of cash.

During her meal, she'd greeted no fewer than six other patrons and passersby, once or twice asking to pet a happy-to-be-out-and-about pooch. Having her fill of socialization and furbaby encounters, she decided it was time to head back to the boardwalk and see what was cooking on the vacation home front.

As she strode back, enjoying the sunny walk, she found some more dogs to pet and more island folk to chat with. Everyone seemed happy. Easy, breezy. Island life was a good one. Of this, Tatum was certain.

She continued along the shoreline of the western coast of the island, studying the lake and thinking about all the life that lived just below the water's surface. The fish and turtles and whatever else Lake Huron played home to.

Mostly, Tatum thought about her pups and her cat. How her mom was treating them. If they had enough water. If they'd gotten their walks.

And what they might think of living in a place like Heirloom Island.

Smirking to herself, Tatum vowed to push the idea away. It was too radical. Too soon. She'd lose credibility with her sisters if she cast such a notion into their consciousness yet.

Biding her time was all Tatum could outwardly do.

But privately, she had a plan.

A plan that would change everything.

19

The plot to mend fences with Darla was going as smoothly as Cadence could have hoped.

First, she'd reined her into planning the party. Of course Cadence didn't need Darla's help. Not only did she have the girls, but Cadence herself had been known to throw a soiree or two. That was the price of marrying into the Van Dam bunch. Hostessing. How could she live in one of the boardwalk houses and *not* throw events?

Naturally, however, Darla didn't know this. And the girls just assumed Cadence was too stricken by grief still to step up to the plate.

Yes, smooth. Everything was as smooth as butter.

Now, Cadence and Darla were getting ready to head across the lake and over one town to the wholesale warehouse. Even with the reunion reduced by half, it still made financial sense to shop in bulk for this one. They could save leftovers. It was the smart thing to do, and even Darla agreed.

However, Tatum was missing, and they couldn't well just take off without at least touching base.

"She's not answering her phone," Darla complained, her own cell cradled limply in her hand as they stood together in the living room.

"I bet she's at the Bait Shop," Mila offered. "It's the place to be."

"The Bait Shop?" Darla made a face.

"It's not what you think. It's the island's version of a market. They have *everything*. You could get what you need there, you know."

"We need a lot more than the Bait Shop would have on hand," Cadence pointed out. "And it's impolite to deplete them, anyway."

"Are we taking the ferry? Maybe we'll bump into her," Darla pointed out.

Mila, who lounged on the sofa, said, "You have too much to bring back. It'll be awkward."

Mila was right. Whenever they'd done big shopping trips, they'd taken the Bayliner, a beautiful, well-cared for cuddy cabin powerboat the family had used for over twenty years now.

"We could take *Katarina*," Cadence suggested, chewing her lower lip anxiously.

Darla raised an eyebrow. "*Katarina*?"

"Hendrik's boat." Cadence hated taking the boat. Not only did it represent Hendrik, but it represented his past, too. Even when he was alive, she had a hang-up. Ridiculous, really, but there it was.

After all, no matter how dead Katarina Van Dam was, her spirit really had lived on. And even *if* the girls had come to accept Cadence as their own, she'd never *really* be their mother.

Then again, Katarina had never *really* been Hendrik's wife, either. This was a deeply held suspicion. One Cadence couldn't shake loose, try as she might.

Katarina, the boat, represented all of this. For she was less a boat and more a, well, *ghost.*

She wanted to take it back. And she tried. "We *could* take the ferry, though. They allow luggage, so they'll allow a few boxes of party essentials. And Darla, you're right. We'll surely bump into Tatum this way."

"I can wait for Tatum here," Mila offered innocently as an angel.

"Let me ask you this," Darla interjected. "Which will make my headache worse? A ferry ride or a speedboat ride?"

"*Katarina* isn't a speedboat. It's a cabin boat. But, anyway, definitely the ferry," Mila answered.

Cadence silently seethed. "Fine. We'll take *Katarina*," she gave in, throwing her hands up, defeated. "Mila, when Tatum comes around, let her know where we are. And if the guests need anything—"

"I know, *I know*," Mila whined. "I'll take care of it."

Cadence smiled and squeezed Mila's hand as she moved across the living room to the back door. "Thanks, sweetheart." She could always count on the youngest of the three to help. It's what had made Mila a teacher's pet. But the good kind. Not the annoying kind. The *real* kind.

"We'll have to launch," Cadence told Darla once they were descending the deck stairs down to the boardwalk that crossed the house. "Have you ever launched a boat?"

Darla shrugged. "Once or twice. But I'm more of a beached whale when it comes to watersports."

Cadence smirked. "Well, get ready. Every argument Hendrik and I ever had would begin and end with launching the goldarn boat."

And that was the honest truth. Anyone who wasn't a fisherman or a regular sailor on Heirloom—anyone who only ever took out a boat for leisure, rather—knew the trials and tribulations of launching a boat with one's spouse. Curse words spewed down like rain.

Now, Cadence didn't have the luxury of chewing out Hendrik. She'd have to talk Darla through the launch. She'd have to feign patience and hold her tongue with any and every misstep.

"I actually had to do this for a play *years* ago, if you can believe that."

Cadence looked at her sister with surprise. "You're joking."

"Nope." Darla followed her to the Suburban, to which Cadence worked on hitching the boat trailer. She continued to explain as Cadence fussed and futzed. "It was a postmodern take on Noah and the Ark. All very metaphoric, but they had us haul in a skiff and launch it into a wet set—that's what we called the pool they designed for the stage. We had to dock it each day, haul it out, relaunch the next day. That way we could clean the set and the skiff. It was all very *method*," she added with dramatic emphasis. "Which means the crew had to learn to maneuver a boat every which way." Darla shrugged and attached the electrical plug, finishing the last step of the hitching process.

Color Cadence impressed, because she was.

"Let's do this," she said, hopping into the driver's seat.

The next half hour got them all the way through the process. It was the fastest Cadence had ever launched before. At least, with someone other than Hendrik. Even despite their launching fights, they could work quickly together.

With the Suburban parked and locked and the boat tied off and Darla standing in it, Cadence joined her and started the engine.

Nothing.

She tried again.

Again, nothing.

Swallowing, she slid her gaze to the passenger seat, where Darla had been sitting, looking comfortable. Darla shifted in her seat. She leaned forward. "What?"

Cadence tried again.

Still, *nothing*.

"The engine won't start."

"It won't *start*?" Darla all but scratched her head.

"Tell me you practiced starting the boat, too, on that so-called wet set."

Darla shook her head. "No. It wasn't a power boat." Her face lost its triumphant gleam. "Turn the ignition while you hit the gas," she suggested.

Cadence didn't know about that. She'd never had to do it before. Could she break something? She hesitated, then pulled her sunglasses down her nose, squinting around. A line of sweat broke out along her spine. She was immediately miserable.

"We should take the ferry," she grumbled.

Darla groaned. "Here, let me try."

But even Darla didn't have the magic needed to bring *Katarina* back to life.

"The ferry?" she asked, half moaning.

All her life, Darla had been cursed with motion sickness. Cadence remembered this since she was a kid, beginning to take Mom's seat in the front, the AC blasting her in the face while the rest of them froze in the second seat of Dad's Montero as they drove cross-country to visit this relation or that.

Cadence pulled her glasses off all the way, stood at the bow, and shielded her eyes from the morning sun. She looked hard across the boardwalk, hoping to see a familiar face. One of Hendrik's fishing buddies or sailing pals.

Though none of them materialized, another figure *did*.

A man. Capable, yes. A boating man. A man who, in fact, owned his very own boat.

Cadence pointed and slapped at Darla's shoulder. "Look."

"What?" Darla twisted, still irritated, and followed her sister's gesture.

Cadence pushed her index finger through the air, pointing directly at him. "Mason."

20

D arla stood and narrowed in on him. Mason was heading down the back stairs of Liesel's rented house, straight for the boardwalk.

Alone.

She took a gulp of air. "Maybe he can help?"

Cadence agreed readily. "Either that or we take the ferry."

"Not the ferry. Please," Darla begged. She'd had enough nausea for one trip, thankyouverymuch.

Cadence held her wide-brimmed straw hat down on her head and threw up her other hand, waving in broad sweeps to catch his eye. It didn't take long. He waved back, and from their short distance, it was easy to catch the broad smile painted on his face.

Darla pushed down the swirling sensation in her stomach.

"Everything okay?" Mason's grin sank into a look of concern.

"I hate to pester you," Cadence answered, "but our

boat won't start. Do you know any quick fixes for this sort of thing?"

Darla cringed. Cadence wasn't exactly selling them as competent.

He scratched his jaw then jumped right in from the dock, taking Cadence's place at the helm. "When's the last time you took her out?"

"Out? The boat, you mean?" Cadence asked.

Darla burned with subtle embarrassment.

"Hmm." Cadence tapped her chin with a finger. "It's been a while."

"Do you have somewhere to be? I can take a look, but it'll be a process. Have to get her back onto the trailer. The whole nine yards. I know a mechanic at the marina who might be willing to come out, just in case I can't figure it out but—" He scratched his jaw again. "Like I said. If you have to be somewhere soon..." His voice trailed off.

Darla wasn't sure what Cadence's time frame was, really. She still had over a day to get everything shopped. Was the boat repair more pressing? "Do you want to just take the ferry?" Darla asked. "And deal with this later?"

"We're not on a time crunch," Cadence reasoned. "But..."

"It's the reunion party," Darla offered Mason an explanation. "We're headed to the wholesale warehouse up the shore to get food and supplies."

"I was just heading over to Birch Harbor myself." Surprise colored his face as Mason acted all but shocked to know they shared this coincidence.

Cadence clasped her hands together as though he'd already offered a ride.

But he hadn't. And Darla had better manners than to make assumptions.

"Oh!" she said, cutting Cadence off at the pass before she embarrassed them both. The thing to do was to put it back on the person with control of the offer. *Not* presume that an offer was to be made. "Cadence," she addressed her sister, "you're right. We can take the ferry."

"The ferry? Don't be ridiculous. It's not fun to lug stuff onto the *Birch Bell*, quaint as the ol' girl is. I'll give you a lift."

But what about the whole driving part of their expedition? He'd be stuck with them.

To Darla that wasn't a bad thing.

To Cadence, it might be.

To Mason, it would *certainly* be.

Darla replied, "You'd be stuck with us while we shop."

"I could go for a grossly oversize tub of beef jerky. I mean, it wouldn't hurt for us to have some snacks on hand, right?"

Cadence visibly stiffened. "I put snacks in the rental."

"You did!" Mason agreed, hands up in the air. "I just mean...something other than hummus and organic corn chips?"

Darla laughed, and the tension broke. She elbowed Cadence in the side. "What do you say?"

Cadence gave Mason a hard look. "Are you sure? I wouldn't want you to get bogged down by two old broads."

Darla's eyes bulged clear out of her head. "Speak for

yourself!" she chided her sister. It seemed necessary to clear the air on that one, so she immediately followed by giving Mason a sharp look and adding, "I'm only thirty-five." *Only* wasn't the right modifier there, but it was too late.

Mason chuckled and pushed a hand through his hair. "I'm thirty-six."

Her breath hitched. He didn't need to say that. He did not need to say that.

But there it was.

He'd said it.

Jumping back out on the dock, Mason reached a hand down. Darla stood in front of Cadence, so of course it was only logical she take it. But by the time she did and found herself on dry dock with him, Cadence had already hauled her own self out of the boat behind them.

A grin curled her thirty-seven-year-old lips.

21

When she'd finally made her way back to the boardwalk houses, Tatum considered stopping first at Liesel's rental, just to check in. But that wasn't Tatum's place.

Still, she paused again at the second house, her lodgings. It loomed a little higher than the first. A little more modern, despite the fact that all three houses were built around the same time. Decades and decades ago. They'd held up well. The Cape Cod–style timelessness and, even if not low maintenance, well maintained.

She sucked in a breath, nervous to pitch her grand idea to Darla, whom she'd already tricked once on this trip.

Talking to Cadence would be no better. Tatum had kept her even more in the dark.

But even so, that third boardwalk house sat a little taller than the first two, yet. Brighter. It called to her.

Following her gut, Tatum passed her own vacay digs and made her way to the longest staircase from the boardwalk, the one that led to Cadence's—and the Van Dam girls'—back deck.

She rapped once on the back door, willing Lotte to appear first. Of the three daughters, Lotte came across as the easiest going. The coolest. The sort to be excited about Tatum's irrational decision.

It was little Mila instead. The smallest in stature *and* the blondest—her hair a wispy white—Mila seemed even younger than she already was. Maybe that could work in Tatum's favor. She could sort of rally the troops around her cause, and then *strike.*

"Hi!" Tatum's voice trilled a touch too cheery, but Mila returned the greeting, anyway.

"You *just* missed them."

"Missed them?" Missed who? Could Mila read it on her face like a big, fat billboard: Now showing! Tatum Sageberry in her latest role as an unstable looney. Costarring Tatum's band of hapless mutts and that one fussy cat that any real loon always totes around!

"Your sisters. You're looking for Cadence and Darla, right?" She stepped aside, and Tatum took that as her cue to enter the house. She paused on the rug that ran the length of the French doors.

"Oh, right." Tatum made a show of being bashful and uncertain. "May I come in?"

"Come in!" Mila assumed her position as the hostess, even now that she was officially living *back home.*

Tatum knew what it was to live at home past the age of eighteen. It used to be, as her parents said at the time, that kids never did that. They left at eighteen and forged a life of their own, marrying and popping out a string of cherubs in their three-bedroom-two-bath on Elm Street. *The American Dream*, her dad called it. *The real world*, her mother would say.

Tatum capitalized on this commonality. "How's day two?" she started, following Mila to the kitchen. Ah, yes. The *kitchen*—the hub of any happy family.

"Day two?" Mila reached in the fridge for a jug of yesterday's iced tea and set about pouring two glasses.

Accepting hers, Tatum explained. "Living back home. I mean, I know it's not exactly the same, since Cadence is your stepmom, but *still.*" She hesitated meaningfully. "I had to move back home after I dropped out of college."

Mila's eyes grew wide. Tatum expected this. No matter the audience, there was always a *reaction* to such news. Tatum sort of enjoyed it. It told her a lot about the person receiving the news. How they grew up. What they valued. What they believed. Mila swallowed her first gulp of tea. "You *dropped out.*" She glanced around like they might get in trouble, but a little smile broke out along her lips.

"It wasn't for me." Tatum lifted an eyebrow. "Lots of things are...*not for me.*"

Mila's expression turned inscrutable. "Yeah," she said after a beat. "I think I know what you mean."

Giving the conversation a little breathing room, Tatum enjoyed her drink, allowing her mind to float back to the kids at her mom's house. She'd chatted briefly with Pat that morning, setting the third phase of Operation Boardwalk House into motion deftly. Subtly. With Pat, you had to be deft. Subtle. Too much of a matriarch, that woman. Refused to let her daughters make mistakes. She'd rather they shoot a clear path toward victory, avoid heartache and hard lessons and all those things that taught a woman how to deal with *life*.

Tatum studied Mila for another beat. "School." She shook her head, like she knew. Heck, she *did* know.

"It's not that I don't like school, it's...that I don't like my classes."

"You're studying to be a teacher? Like Cadence?"

"She always said I'd be such a good teacher. And she told me I'd love the summer vacations. Which I would. I like my time off, that's true."

"As if other jobs don't allow for time off?" Tatum snorted. It was so like Cadence to follow in Pat's footsteps. Do as I do. And as I say. And life will be just *grand*.

Pat was a teacher. Nothing wrong with that, no. And there was nothing wrong with Cadence becoming one, either. She liked it well enough. She was good. And look what it had afforded her in the end! The sort of life of which teachers could hardly dream. Ha!

"Well, she's right. I mean, what other job gives you downtime?"

"That depends on what downtime looks like to you," Tatum reasoned. "I remember when we were growing up, every afternoon was spent in my mother's classroom. Cleaning chalkboards—whiteboards later on—and thumbing through kids' books for an hour or two until she'd finally caught up for the day and prepped for the next. Oh, and summers? Mom cleaned houses to make ends meet." Tatum smirked. So much for time off.

In her adjacent barstool, Mila shrank back. "Yeah." She sighed. "That's sort of what I'm afraid of. I mean, teaching is *cool*, but what I'm really into is marine biology.

Cadence says I'll have the summers off, and I can do marine biology stuff then. But...what about other times of the year? And what if I need a part-time job? *Before*, I didn't, but now..." The girl's voice trailed off.

"You mean the money issue. With your dad?" Tatum figured that was the point of reference. "I mean, if you really want to teach, you could literally teach marine biology. Or you could swing a part-time gig on the lake or on an ocean somewhere for when you have time off."

"But at that point," Mila argued, "why wouldn't I just become a marine biologist? Then I'm doing what I love *for* my job."

It wasn't Tatum's place to confirm that Mila was more logical than Cadence.

Or was it? And if it was, then would that help to win Mila over? Or push her away?

Then again, did Tatum really *want* to win Mila over? Or did she just want to be a good friend? A confidante? Someone the girl could look to for solid advice?

"Sometimes you don't really know what you love to do until you do it, though. And even more than that, you might want to do something...but in a different way." She shook her head and rolled her eyes at herself. "That makes no sense. Sorry."

"No, I think it does," Mila answered, a thoughtful look in her eyes.

Tatum thought back to her own brief college stint.

Mila asked, "What was it you studied? And what was it you wanted to do?"

"For me, it was a matter of *how*."

Mila squinted at her.

Tatum explained. "Animals. It's always been animals for me. So, naturally, that started out as a vet thing, right? I mean, all dog-lover kids want to be veterinarians when they grow up. Right?"

Mila shrugged. "I guess so?"

"What"—Tatum eyed her—"you don't love dogs?"

Mila widened her eyes, affronted. Her hand flew to her chest defensively. "I *love* dogs. I love all animals! That's why I want to study them. Except, not so much the furry ones as the slippery ones."

Tatum beamed back. "You and I are more alike than I realized." She lifted an eyebrow. "Except why are you giving teaching a consideration? Simply for summer breaks?"

Mila seemed to mull this over. "I guess because Cadence has always said I'd be a good teacher. She never said anything like that to my sisters, you know?"

Tatum did. She'd grown up on the opposite end of the spectrum. Being the one who didn't get to play favorite to a parent. Whereas Cadence was Mom's preferred and closest daughter, and Darla was Dad's, Tatum was more like a family pet. Her parents and sisters fretted and cooed over her, but she was still, well, just a *pet*. Never her mother's protégé. Never her father's daddy's girl.

"Sure, I do," Tatum replied at last. No wonder Cadence adored Mila. Mila was moldable and shapeable and *normal*, too. She went along to get along. Unlike the writer Fay and singer Lotte.

But what about their *real* mother? Had she, too, taken much interest in the girls? And why did Tatum fear the answer was no?

22

They were seated at the bow, both Cadence and Darla.

Mason drove like Hendrik, which made Cadence feel sad.

Not halfway across and Darla shot up. A look of panic streaked her face.

Mason killed the engine and rushed to join them, Cadence now at her younger sister's side, rubbing her back like Mom would have.

Darla bent over the side and full-on wretched into the lake. Cadence waved Mason off, entirely aware of how embarrassing such a situation was.

He backed away and called up asking if she needed a water—*anything*?

"That'd be great," Darla responded, easing back to her seat. "I'm so sorry. It's the ride. The motion. I'm so sorry."

"No, don't be!" Mason rejoined them and passed her a water.

Cadence discreetly removed a mint from her handbag and passed it Darla. "You sure you're not sick? We can go home." She used the word *home*, even though home had lately taken on a different meaning entirely.

Before Hendrik's death, home was *him*.

Now it was, well, it was just the house. The house that she once again shared with the girls. Which was fine. It was all *fine*.

"I'm sure I'm not. I feel fine otherwise. I mean..." She pressed a hand to her head. "I could use a Tylenol."

Cadence again sprang to action, plucking a leopard-print pill pouch from her bag and dropping two white tablets into Darla's open hand. "Travel can be exhausting. It's the main reason Hendrik and I stopped doing very much of it. I know, lots of people want to *see the world*! Experience *life*. Sometimes, though, you can get your taste of life just as well on the sofa with a good film. Or a good book, of course." She winked at Mason like he might understand, but Cadence didn't know him from Adam.

Even so, there was a boyish quality in him. Maybe the reddish hair. The speedboat? The easy way and quick-to-get-alongness about him? He reminded her of a little brother she never had.

"I used to be big on travel," Mason offered. They were drifting now. The subtle current of Lake Huron casting them up and down along the shore of Birch Harbor. He wasn't the sort to rush a seasick woman into recovery. He took his time.

Cadence eyed Mason as Mason eyed Darla.

She ran the back of her hand over her mouth after a

final swig of water. "Really?" Darla threw a glance at Cadence. It was meant as a sisterly glance. There was something in it, but Cadence wasn't sure what it meant, and she could kick herself for that.

Here they were, primed for bonding, and Cadence couldn't read her own sister.

She looked harder, searching Darla's features for some clue, but she came up empty. Then, she leaned back. "Really?" Cadence prompted Mason without taking her eyes off her sister. "What? Did you have to settle down?"

A smirk lifted his cheeks. "Something like that." But he was quick to explain. "That was a past life."

"Do you want to travel again?" Darla asked. She appeared better. Her color was back. Her mood brighter.

Feeling something akin to a third wheel suddenly, Cadence wondered if she ought to slip into the driver's seat and play chaperone.

"I'm traveling now," Mason answered, slapping his thighs, standing, and cutting Cadence off before she popped up. He held his arms wide and made his way back to the steering wheel. "Heirloom Island." He fell into the seat, twisted, and then flashed a broad grin at them both.

He didn't have to ask if Darla was ready.

Neither did Cadence.

All anyone needed to do was take one look at her, post-wretch and all...the woman was simply glowing.

23

When they made it to shore, Darla let out a breath she'd been holding. Maybe it was because she feared she'd get sick again.

Maybe it was because she was riding at the bow of Mason's boat, her dark hair whipping back like a rope.

Her sister in the seat opposite.

Now, as Mason tied them off to a berth, Darla and Cadence loitered on the dock awkwardly. Her car sat waiting in the long-term parking section of the squat lot beyond the marina office. She supposed his did, too. But once he hopped up beside them, he rubbed his hands together. "My lunch date isn't until, well, lunch." He guffawed, and Darla's knees weakened at it.

"Come with us," she said, fire in her eyes.

She could feel Cadence staring at her, but who cared?

Hunter was old news. Darla was starting over. Tackling her bucket list, right?

And who said she couldn't add more items to it? Who said that ten was a magic number?

And anyway, of the top three on her list, she'd still only managed to tick off half of one.

It wasn't as though a summer fling—or even just a summer crush—would get in the way of all the things Darla wanted to do with her life.

And, besides all that, Cadence would be hanging around like a chaperone. A chaperone with whom Darla still had a bone to pick, to boot.

"I'd love to," Mason answered.

And just like that, they moved from the boat to the car and took off up Harbor Highway, following Mason's smooth directions and Cadence's chest clutching at any turn or stop that was a tad too sharp.

In half an hour, they'd arrived. The warehouse looming high in the late morning sky.

"Got the list?" Cadence asked as the trio climbed out and made their way in, Cadence flashing her warehouse club credentials at the gatekeeper.

Darla passed it to her sister, and as soon as they were inside, Mason murmured something about samples and meeting back at the front then promptly disappeared.

"He's like a kid," Cadence hissed once they were alone again.

"A kid?" Darla frowned. "What are you talking about?"

"He's excitable and fearless, and he's silly. Like a kid or something."

Darla had gotten an entirely different impression. She followed Cadence to the paper products section. "I think he's a breath of fresh air. He doesn't take life too seriously." Unlike Hunter. Hunter with his football-game shouting and apartment rules. No girls on the sofa during the game. Appetizers had to be ordered according to his specifications and at just the right time.

And then there was hunting season.

Oh, yes. Hunter was a hunter, of course. The gear and the planning. It all felt a little too much like a murder plot as opposed to a gaming tradition. And much, *much* less than what hunting really ought to be: securing meat for the winter. No, Hunter was in it far more for the trophy— the rack—than anything else.

Only now, catching a glimpse of Mason chatting with a woman in a hairnet and plastic gloves who was dishing out two-inch squares of lasagna in paper cups, did any of that stuff about Hunter percolate.

Cadence plopped a yard-long pack of paper napkins into the cart and swung it around, away from Mason and the lasagna samples and down the other way. "If you ask me, he's not giving us the full story."

"Huh?" Darla edged closer to her sister, resting a hand on the metal cart. "What are you talking about?"

"He joins up with Liesel and her little brood for this family reunion, *despite* the fact that his own immediate family bails. And he teaches at the high school? He lives in Birch Harbor? Why spend the money and stay in the rental?"

At this, Darla was offended. "Well, I'd like to think maybe he was a little...I don't know...*intrigued*? Maybe he's up for adventure. He said he likes to travel. And he seems adventurous."

"I wonder what Hendrik would have him pegged for." Cadence tugged at her black top like she was hot.

Darla wasn't following. "Hendrik? What do you mean? You think Hendrik could have seen through Mason?"

"Hendrik had a nose for character. And the truth." Cadence threw her shoulders back and down and shook her short hair off her neck.

Darla couldn't help it. It was a softball, lobbed perfectly center above the plate in slow motion. "A nose for character, huh? I suppose having a nose for character is different than *having* character."

Cadence narrowed an icy gaze on her. "What?"

"Well, I hate to say this, Cadence. But I figured you knew how it looked."

"How *what* looked?" Cadence froze, her knuckles white on the cart handle.

"How it looked when he married his daughter's teacher...not even a year after his wife's death."

24

Tatum didn't tell Mila her plan.

By the time their conversation wound down, it felt irrelevant. It was clear to Tatum that what Mila needed was an example, sure. Someone other than her stepmother to give her life tips. But was that someone really Tatum?

Maybe.

Maybe not.

Anyway, the best way for someone to learn was by example. Tatum could rant and rave all she wanted about following one's dream. That would mean nothing, however, until she did it.

So, after Mila left to reexamine her class schedule for the following fall, Tatum took off again.

This time, for the hills.

She packed a sack lunch of Ritz crackers and a few slices of American cheese. A can of Diet Coke, for good measure. Tatum wasn't much of a fan of Diet Coke, but she reasoned it might make sense to bring caffeine. Give her a little midday jolt and ensure she arrived safely back on the boardwalk with some energy left.

Her travel backpack now set, off she took on foot into the wilds of Heirloom Island. If such wilds existed.

Without much more than a loose mental map— points of reference derived from a brief Google Maps search of her locale—she decided to take the way that wound beyond the boardwalk. Where the boardwalk might go if someone had the motivation to continue it.

This way proved to be a bit of a workout. A pathless walk over sandy dunes and weedy patches of lake beach had her feeling aimless.

No houses appeared to exist on the southwestern tip of Heirloom. Instead, the area was thick with Michigan forest. Evergreens and sugar maples grew densely, obscuring Tatum's view to the innermost segment of Heirloom.

She wondered how quickly she could become lost in there, and decided it was best to stay along the coast and walk as far as her legs would take her. Then, she'd sit and eat, take a break. Head back.

Unless...she happened to find what she was looking for.

25

Cadence didn't have to explain herself to Darla. No, sirree.

Cadence didn't have to explain that she fell in love with her student's father. She didn't have to explain the chain of events. The Van Dam history.

None of it.

Especially after Darla had made what many might consider to be a poor decision. Breaking off nuptials said volumes about Darla. About what she *really* valued and how she strung people along to get it.

And, still, Cadence *knew* how her own marriage looked. Boy, howdy, did she *ever*. She knew, and yet, she didn't care.

And neither had Hendrik.

And most surprising of all, neither did the girls.

Because what the Van Dams knew was what the rest of the world did *not*.

Katarina Van Dam had ended their marriage five years earlier. She'd ended it, and she'd run away. She'd run away from her husband and her daughters and her *life*.

And she'd left Hendrik with the girls on the island, creating stories to glaze over the fact that their family matriarch was out of the picture. Nothing could be worse for a family like the Van Dams than personal shame, after all.

So, they *pretended*. For five whole years, they pretended. Until one day, the pretending came to a screeching halt.

Mila could no longer stand the torment of her friends —*you don't even have a mom*, that sort of teasing—and wanted to switch schools.

And then, not a month later, Hendrik stepped his foot into a parent-teacher conference at St. Mary's and set his sights on Miss Cadence Sageberry.

AFTER FINISHING THE SHOPPING TRIP, they spent another ten minutes tracking down Mason, who, predictably now, had started his second lap of sampling. He was back at the lasagna cart. Only this time, lasagna had been swapped out for pink lemonade.

Thirsty herself, Cadence accepted a plastic cup and downed the stuff. But it didn't quite get the quenching done.

As they moved through the checkout, Cadence wondered aloud if Mason knew of any good places for lunch at the marina. "Somewhere with a great Arnold Palmer maybe?" Cadence already had a few answers in her pocket. The Harbor Deli. Fiorillo's. So on and so forth.

But Mason offered something else. "You should join my buddy and me," Mason said, his attention directed not to Cadence, but to Darla. "We're going to grab a bite and a drink at Birch Tree Brewery. It's a dive. Inland."

Darla answered, prim and coy, "Oh, we'd hate to crash your friend time."

He laughed. "Only girls have friend time. Guys hang out. And, anyway, Rip would never turn down lunch with a pair of pretty ladies."

For whatever reason, his compliment struck Cadence as awkward. *Pretty lady* was somehow lesser than *beautiful woman*. Or even *cute girl*. But it wasn't just that that stopped her in her tracks in the parking lot. "Rip?"

Hardly anyone in modern America was named Rip. Even in this Dutch slice of America, the greater Birch Harbor area.

But Cadence knew a Rip. No way could there be more than one of him.

"Rip, yeah." Mason's eyes grew wider. "Oh, geez! You must *know* Rip. How could I be so dense!" He slapped his palm on his forehead.

Darla giggled.

Giggled.

Cadence picked back up walking, and they followed her, Mason pushing the cart and Darla still gripping one side of it. She answered into the wind. "If it's Rip Van Dam, of course I do."

She didn't glance back to see their reactions.

Once the car was loaded and they were buckled and

ready to roll, Darla turned the ignition and looked at Cadence. "So, who's Rip? Is that his real name? How do you know him?" Her chattiness had come out of the blue, overshadowing the ongoing attitude that Darla had arrived with. Satisfied to have male companionship. Only satisfied *when* she had male companionship. Just like their mother.

"Yeah." Cadence rolled her eyes. "Rip Van Dam the Fourth, or something ridiculous."

Mason asked, "You're related to him, then?"

"All Van Dams on either Heirloom Island or in Birch Harbor are related. Curse of the Lake, I call it." She hesitated then twisted in her seat. "Aren't you from here? How do you not know that?"

Mason shrugged. "I wasn't born here. I didn't even grow up here. I only started teaching this last winter."

Cadence knew that Mr. Acton was new to the school. A steal. A valued recruit, by all local accounts. Even Mila had mentioned he came across like some sort of teaching legend that Birch Harbor was lucky to score. But he was an Acton. Actons came from Birch Harbor. They ran the lighthouse back in the day. They had roots there.

"Your family is, though," Cadence confirmed.

"Yeah. Family is. Dad moved away after high school. Married. Stayed gone." He chuckled.

Darla stole a look in her rearview mirror. "Why'd you come back?"

They were met with silence at first.

"Turn left here," he instructed Darla. Then, "Fresh start. Job came up. One of my cousins told me about it.

She teaches at the high school. Knew about my"—he cleared his throat—"situation."

"What situation?" Cadence and Darla jinxed one another then shared a smile.

It was less Mason's personal scandal, however, that enchanted the sisters.

And more the fact that, for the first time since Darla and Tatum had arrived, the sisters had found something in common. Something to delight over together. For the first time, they could listen to someone else's drama.

Not their own.

And *that* was something.

Darla pulled into a shallow parking lot along the side of Harbor Highway.

An old neon sign flickered dimly in the daylight. Birch Tree Brewery. Best Burger in Birch Town!

"Birch Town?" she asked.

As they got out of the car, Mason explained. "The guys who started this place tried to break away. You know, like how the South tried to secede back in the Civil War?"

Darla lifted an eyebrow. "This sounds concerning."

He chuckled and waved her off. "They didn't like how incestuous the area had become. Or, maybe, how it always was. You'll find lots of descendants who hang out here, but also lots of newcomers. I suppose that's why I like it. And Rip, too."

"Rip." Darla slid her eyes to her sister. "Is he a black sheep?"

"Rip is...*Rip*." Cadence sighed.

Sounded to Darla that Rip was the Van Dam equivalent of Tatum.

Mason held the door open, and the women stepped into a dimly lit, almost empty café-bar-restaurant.

Darla half wished it was just her and Mason, but then...she still needed to pin Cadence down. That's what she came to do, after all. At least, in part.

As for a summer crush? That wasn't on her list, and Darla *had* to stick to the list.

They sat, joining a stocky, quiet-but-jovial fellow about the same age as Darla and Mason. His dark, curly hair was cropped close to his head. His face a ruddy red. Crystalline blue eyes and a smile that didn't seem like it'd ever slip away.

Darla liked him right away. It seemed like Cadence did, too. She lightened up, giving in to a bear hug from the shorter man.

This was a sight for sore eyes, and Darla couldn't help but admire the funny bond. And question it. Was this who Cadence had become in the last decade? A local? A family member to people Darla didn't know? It seemed strange.

"Rip, this is my sister Darla." Cadence gestured, and Rip took Darla's hand in his and gave it a hearty shake.

"I've heard a *lot* about you," he said, his grin growing impossibly wider.

Darla blinked. "Oh?"

"*All* good things." He winked.

Darla's smile fell away, and she took a step backward, landing almost in Mason's lap.

He startled, and she yelped, and then Cadence laughed loudly.

"That's Tatum you're thinking of," she said between wheezes. "*Not* Darla."

"Gee, thanks." Darla wasn't sure whether to laugh or apologize to Mason. His hands found their way to her waist, gentlemanly moving her aside. But then, could such a touch ever be gentlemanly? Her stomach swung up to her throat and down like a bungee cord. "I'll take a glass of water," she announced to the waiter, the lone employee of the would-be contrarian tavern.

"Water?" Cadence shook her head and plucked a menu from the table. "Make it two Arnold Palmers. In Birch Harbor, you drink one of three things: iced tea, lemonade, or a bit of both." She gave a short nod to the waiter, then Mason ordered the same before he left.

"So." Darla took the seat Mason offered her, and he sat in the spot next to his friend, Rip, who was unbothered by the mix-up, unlike Darla. She directed her attention to Cadence. "You've told Rip about Tatum?"

Cadence made a choking noise.

"Tatum?" Mason asked. He cocked his head to Rip. "Tatum?"

"Look!" Cadence slapped her hands on the table. "It's *nothing*. Rip missed our wedding. He was out of the country. But he's been back awhile, and he comes and helps with repairs from time to time. He saw a picture of Tatum I had on the fridge."

"The one with the dogs," Rip added.

"Right. The one where Tatum is posing with her dogs. It's a studio photo. She got it done at Sears or JCPenney. I forget." Cadence rolled her eyes. "Anyway, he pointed it out because Tatum is standing behind a draped table, and you can't see her lower half so—"

By this point, Cadence was laughing so hard she couldn't breathe. Rip, too.

Mason and Darla exchanged a look. He gave her a half grin, and she returned it, remembering his hands on her waist moments earlier. Was there something there? Did he feel it, too?

Or was this what they called the rebound effect? The urge to replace, replace, replace, *recover.*

Regardless, she was silly to make anything of the subtle glances, the touch—Mason's good looks. In a week, she'd be gone. So would he.

Then back to Detroit. To a new one-bedroom apartment and another semester of second-year theater students who had it *all figured out.*

Another round of shared laughter shrilled loudly across the empty space. Cadence roared, "She looked like was missing half her body!"

Rip laughed even louder than Cadence, and Darla crinkled her nose at Mason. "I didn't know he had any other friends than me."

Now it was Darla's turn to laugh, and before she knew it, the four of them were laughing; not at different things, but at the same thing. Over, and again. This story or that. This memory or that. Alternating between inside jokes among Rip and Mason and the parallel tales of Cadence and Darla.

By the time they floated outside and into the sunshine of the early afternoon, Cadence bumped into

Darla, their shoulders colliding before Cadence grabbed Darla's hand, squeezing it warmly.

It was then that Darla wondered, was *this* what it felt like to fix the past? Was it loud and silent all at once?

Was *this* true sisterhood?

And mostly, what happened next?

27

Exhausted and defeated, Tatum trudged downstairs for breakfast the next morning.

She forced one foot in front of the other the whole way, and by the time she arrived in the living room, she saw she was alone—where *was* everyone, anyway?— she sank into a sofa, and succumbed to a fit of sobs. Yes. Sobs.

Just totally sobbed. The sort of sob only women really did. When nothing was wrong and everything was wrong and *oh dang it* why couldn't things just be *right*?

No one was around to see if she was okay. And by no one, Tatum meant her pups. Her cat. Her *family*. Her whole being ached to get back to them, but then, that'd ruin the plan. It'd change everything, and she'd be back to square one.

Tatum went to her backpack and removed the newspaper she'd grabbed from the diner, pressing it open on the bar as she poured herself a glass of milk. Milk would soothe her. Too bad there weren't chocolate chip cookies lying around. That wasn't Cadence's style, though, and as far as Tatum cared, a trip to the market would have to wait another day. She was bone tired.

She cradled her phone in one hand and studied the first number before punching the digits to life.

It rang.

Rang.

Rang.

Answering machine.

Tatum left a message and moved on to the next.

Again, nothing.

By the time she'd made it to the fifth and final phone number she'd circled, Tatum had talked to exactly zero people and five answering machines.

It was Saturday morning, right? Saturday was still like a workday in the human world? At least, it was in Detroit. In Detroit, you could take care of any business on a Saturday. From the bank to a stopover at Urgent Care.

So, why no responses?

"It's Saturday!" Tatum screamed to herself.

But she wasn't alone.

"Yes." Darla appeared from veritably nowhere. "It's Saturday," she repeated slowly, her gait matching the rhythm of her answer and the wariness on her features.

"Oh." Tatum's tears dried instantly. The bellows from the base of her chest evaporated. "I was just—"

"It's okay." Darla shook the cautious attitude and joined Tatum on the sofa. "My feelings have changed about our stay, too."

Tatum looked at her, confused. "They have?" Tatum's

feelings hadn't *changed*. What? Did Darla think she wanted to leave now?

Sighing, Darla's expression turned serious. "Yeah." She blinked and shifted to face Tatum. "Do you think—" Her eyes fell closed and she squeezed them shut. "Never mind."

"No, *what*?" Tatum asked.

"No, really. You want to leave. In a week, I'll feel the same. I'll be ready."

Tatum's heart skipped a beat. "Wait. *Darla*. Are you... are you saying you want to stay?"

Darla peered through one eye. "Define *stay*."

"Stay. Stay beyond a week. Like...rent a place, maybe."

Her sister's words spilled out fast. "We'd have to make money."

"We'd find jobs." Tatum's eyes were wild now.

"We'd both chip in." Darla's eyes were wild, too.

"We could stay—" Tatum started, but it wasn't Darla who finished her sentence.

It was Mason, appearing shirtless with nothing more than boardshort trunks on and a beach towel looped around his neck. "Stay here?"

"Where's here?" Tatum and Darla asked in tandem.

"*Here*. In this boardwalk house."

28

Sunday arrived, and Cadence was abuzz with new energy.

The event really wasn't the be-all and end-all. Cadence had teaching. She'd have an income. She would.

But every extra bit would help. It would help keep the other houses through dry spells. It would just *help*. Keep things as they *were*. Cadence *needed* things to be as they *were*.

Beyond all that? Well, Cadence *liked* to put on events. She liked to play party planner and hostess and tweak the fanned-out edges of a set of pretty paper napkins and tug a flower into place in its arrangement. She loved all of that, of course. More than teaching.

Teaching had just been Cadence's job. Maybe, sometimes, her calling. But it's what she did. What she was always going to do. Just like her mother.

And come August, she'd be doing it all over again.

Sigh.

"Lotte!" Cadence called up the staircase. "It's time!"

Time. Time to set up. Time to get ready. *Really* get ready. Not the getting ready that had happened over the previous two days.

Lotte *and* Mila skipped down the stairs from their bedrooms like good soldiers. And they *were*, too.

Fay, on the other hand.

"Where's Fay?"

"At the Bait Shop making copies of the agenda," Mila answered.

"She means *program*," Lotte emphasized. "And by the way, I can't help set up."

Cadence froze. "What? We need your help."

"The guys and I are going to rehearse first. And, anyway, we have to set *our* stuff up, too."

"I thought they were—" Cadence just shook her head. "Okay. Whatever. Mila"—she lowered her chin to the spritely blonde—"go next door and ask Darla and Tatum if they can come earlier."

"Earlier than what?" Mila asked, ever the diligent one.

"They weren't coming for a couple of hours, but without Lotte—and without Fay, for that matter—I need them here sooner."

Mila hesitated, but Cadence didn't have time. "Just *go*."

She did, and Lotte left, too, and then it was only Cadence. Alone for one final moment for the day.

She'd gone to early mass. Six o'clock. Makeupless and her freshly blown-out hair tucked into a neat chignon beneath a headscarf, she kept a low profile there, preferring not to draw the attention of others when she looked so not herself.

She still wore the scarf now and wouldn't touch up her hair, get dressed, or add makeup until just before the reunion. Stealing away for fifteen minutes and reemerging as the perfect hostess. That was her goal. But to be the perfect hostess, she first needed to craft the perfect party.

Clapping her hands, she went to the office, a simple, stately room that Hendrik had used for emails and thinking and that Cadence sometimes invaded for wrapping presents or penning notes to girlfriends, designing invitations, that sort of thing.

Now, she'd set up a spare portable AC unit in there in order to keep the flowers chilled. Presently, they sat in orange five-gallon tubs with the right amount of water. Each tub held a different flower and its paired greenery. Yellow roses with baby's breath. Magnolias and eucalyptus. All that was left to do were the arrangements. With six vases planned, she'd need extra hands. Artful ones.

Between Mila, Darla, and Tatum, she wasn't entirely sure who best fit the role.

But Cadence *would* need to assign roles. That was the best way to coordinate these things.

She took to the whiteboard hanging discreetly behind the door and tapped a finger to her lip before plucking the marker from its clip.

Each of her sisters and daughters had a column, but Cadence had waited on adding their tasks.

Until now.

Lotte.

Well, she'd made it easy on Cadence. *Music.*

Done.

Fay.

Cadence knew she could count on Fay for positively nothing that wasn't behind the scenes. And who knew when she'd return from the Bait Shop? That copy machine had to be thirty years old.

She scrawled *Programs, menus* beneath Fay's name. For posterity's sake.

Under Mila, she knew she could take more liberties. *Sweep deck, set tables.*

Darla was trickier. They'd only just come to a tentative, delicate treaty. A loose truce. It'd be best not to shake that, especially before Cadence had fully had the opportunity to make her amends. And vice versa.

Darla got *Flowers.*

This would allow them a little chatting time to boot.

Lastly, Tatum. The wild card. What would Tatum be best suited to? She was affable to a fault. Bubbly to the point of combustion.

Cadence studied the name and all it had meant to her over the years.

Tatum.

Floater sounded too crude, as did waitress or busser.

MC, no. That was Cadence.

Point person?

Hardly.

Surely Tatum was good at something. Good *for* something. But...what?

What could a reunion use that Tatum Sageberry had?

Cadence tapped her finger once again on her lip,

picturing the course of events. The Hannigans. Liesel and Mark. Mason, randomly, perhaps. *Not* the Actons.

Right? Or *were* some going to make an appearance?

She snapped her fingers. She had it.

Mediator.

29

A fter the powwow Darla had with Tatum and Mason the day before, time started to fly.

Things locked into motion like gears, and Darla found herself tracking down a variety of leads. First, on Tatum's behalf.

Then, on her own.

By the end of the day, exhausted from combing local social media pages, Craigslist ads, and Tatum's newspaper from the Island Koken, Darla and Tatum had come to a mutual agreement.

They'd take Mason's advice.

This was, perhaps, the hardest step. Especially for Darla.

While she'd made progress with Cadence, Darla was a long way from being entirely comfortable. Or, even as comfortable as Tatum was. Then again, Tatum was undoubtedly *entirely* comfortable.

Tatum's comfort was the reason Darla demanded *she* be the one to reveal the big news.

It would have to take place after the reunion. Maybe Monday. Or Tuesday. Mondays were hard.

Were Tuesdays any better?

"Hello?"

The voice called through the front door, and Darla twisted away from the kitchen bar to see Mila pushing through, unbothered by the concept of knocking first.

Darla smiled. She liked Mila.

"Come in," she answered, holding up a pot of coffee. "Need a warm-up?"

Mila shook her head. "Cadence says she needs your help. Tatum's, too." Mila glanced around. "Is Mason here, too?"

Darla flushed, stupidly. She'd woken up much earlier —at five. Her daily headaches had become just that— daily. So had the dizziness, although that had turned subtly into a brief nausea, quenched only by Mason's scrambled eggs. Buttery and salty—but not too much of either—she'd awoken that morning praying he'd be up and at 'em again.

And he was.

"M-Mason went on a run," Darla stammered. No reason she should be embarrassed. They'd only had breakfast. And coffee. Just until Darla was herself again. This morning pattern of headache-dizziness-irritability had grown tiresome. But she'd found a cure. In a handsome stranger who was sleeping just down the hall. How very Harlequin of her.

"Oh, well," Mila answered, "that's okay. Just need to get started, you know."

"Started?"

"The reunion." Mila's face went blank. "We're setting up."

"Oh!" Darla dropped her feet from the overstuffed ottoman, swinging them to the floor and squaring them. "Of course."

This was her chance. "You'll go up and wake Tatum, won't you? I'll go next door and get started!" She didn't wait for Mila to respond. That was the trick with subordinates. You led. They followed. And Darla knew how to lead.

Just...not always with Cadence.

That was why she had a plan.

WHEN SHE ARRIVED at the house next door, she pushed inside. A powerful fragrance hit her square in the nose.

Peering around the edge of the door much like Mila had minutes earlier, Darla called into the cavernous house. "Cade?" She waited a beat. "Cadence?"

"In here! The office!"

Darla followed the voice, the scent growing stronger until she poked into the open French doors.

Cadence had a folding table out. On it, six glass vases. Scattered around the table, six orange buckets, each filled with beautiful flowers. Roses, baby's breath...

"Eucalyptus?" she asked, bending to cup her hand beneath a soft green leaf.

Cadence pulled a tablecloth tight, pinching it at the corners. She gave a short nod and a smile then plucked a different flower from another bucket. "And magnolias. I think they work for reunions."

"Gorgeous," Darla said on a breath.

Cadence smirked. "That's the plan. I considered keeping the bouquets separate, I mean separating the flowers. But mixing them looks so pretty."

"Opposites can attract," Darla agreed.

"And anyway," Cadence went on, "are they really so opposite? They're similar. But they complement each other."

The two exchanged a brief look.

Darla lifted a single magnolia to her nose and inhaled. The scent was sharper than she'd expected. Stronger. Something between a lemon and an orange and... She frowned.

"Citrus vanilla?" Cadence asked, reading her mind.

"Or is it honey?" Darla answered.

Cadence just shrugged and held out her hand. "It changes. That's how magnolias are. Their scent depends on their circumstances. I think magnolias are the most ephemeral."

"Transitory," Darla added.

"Mercurial."

Darla laughed lightly. "Fickle."

"They remind me of sisters." Cadence said this with a small smile. A knowing look. "Like us."

Darla picked up a white rose and fondled the stem. "Your wedding really was beautiful," she murmured to Cadence.

A silence came in reply.

Darla looked up, searching her sister's expression.

"You didn't like him." Cadence said it flatly.

Darla shook her head. "I didn't know him."

"You knew he was a man who dated his daughter's teacher. A younger woman," Cadence pointed out. In that moment, she lost some of that wisdom Darla had always seen in her older sister.

"And I knew you weren't interested in marriage," Darla returned. "It just didn't make sense. You...you were always so independent, Cadence. To become a *stereotype*."

30

Tatum awoke with a start.

"Huh?" she slurred, shielding her eyes from the inevitable sunlight that clawed its way between the Roman shutters and through the gauzy curtains meant to keep it out. "Who is it?" she drawled through half sleep.

"Sorry," came a whispered peep. "It's me. Mila. Sorry to wake you."

Tatum dragged herself to a sitting position and pushed her hand through her hair. "Mila." She rubbed her eyes. "Good. Good." It was nonsense coming from her mouth, and though she knew this, she was still fighting through sleep to wake fully. "Not a morning person," she added, her voice raspy. Tatum reached for her water glass. "Come in." She took a swig, swallowing greedily, then drew her legs into a pretzel. "Sit down." She patted the spot on the bed where her feet should be.

Mila perched at the outermost edge.

Tatum stretched her arms up and out, yawned, smiled. "Hi."

Mila giggled. "Hi. Um, I only came in to let you know Cadence was trying to reach you."

"Reach me?" Tatum yawned again then dug her hand beneath the pillow opposite her sleeping spot. She squinted at the screen, yawning for a third time. "Oh, yeah." Giving her head a shake. "Reunion day."

"Anyway," Mila said as she stood, lingering, "I did have one other little thing..."

Sounded like a big thing. "Is this a coffee conversation?"

"A coffee conversation?" Mila looked suspicious. Suspicious or confused.

"Why do I have a feeling you've been mulling over my pearls of wisdom?" Tatum asked back. No question about it. Something Tatum had said to Mila struck a nerve. The sort of nerve that was hard to soothe. The sort that rose up and caused a lot of issues and questions and sleepless nights.

The sort that would no doubt get Tatum in trouble with Cadence. Maybe even Darla, too.

She let out a sigh and prepared to tell Mila to take her advice with a grain of salt.

Instead, Mila's expression hardened. "I'll put a pot on. You get ready."

Mila left, and that was that.

She'd officially become somebody's crazy aunt.

∼

THEY SAT AT THE BAR, Tatum nursing her third mug and Mila sipping orange juice. The kid in her was still alive and well. When had Tatum lost that? Or maybe she hadn't? Maybe she was one of those kids who drank coffee. The twelve-year-old girl who strolled into her sixth-grade classroom with a Starbucks and an attitude, maybe.

"You can't drop out," Tatum said at last.

Mila had given her a list of reasons everything Tatum had said before now rang true. A list of reasons Mila needed to take a break from school to figure out what she wanted to do. Who she wanted to be.

"But I don't want to be a high school teacher. Even a biology one," Mila complained.

Tatum gave her a pointed look. "No whining. It's one thing to give up school because, well, you're never going to be a schoolish person. Like me."

Mila cocked her head.

"It's another to give up school because you're not happy in your current program. You want to work in the water, right? You want to be a scientist?"

Mila nodded.

"Then you need that degree. I knew that to do what I wanted, I didn't need a degree. Mila, the reality is, if you want to support yourself one day by doing what you love, then you have to take all the right steps. Quitting school is the wrong step."

"But not if I go back. Eventually," Mila reasoned.

"What're you going to do in the meantime?" Tatum asked.

"Well, I mean, I figure maybe I can get, like, *experience*.

I could apply at the marina. Or here, at the Bait Shop."

"What'll that do for you? Working at the Bait Shop, I mean?" Tatum smiled, amused.

Mila beamed proudly. "They host scuba classes, you know. That's where I got certified."

"Scuba?" The word gave her a feeling. Reminded her of something. Something important.

Mila cocked her head. "Scuba," she repeated. "You know, it's...diving. Scuba diving."

Tatum shook her head. "Yeah. I know—" Then, it hit her. "Scuba!" she cried, her face stretched in excitement. "Darla! And scuba!"

"Does she dive?" Mila asked, looking stricken. Confused.

"No, but she *wants* to." Tatum came alive. Just the day before, with Mason, they'd concocted this wild scheme. But was it...coming true? Was this the first of any number of good omens? *Darla's list.* "It's on her bucket list." Oops. Were bucket lists things of privacy?

"What else is on her bucket list?" Mila asked. "Did she always want to be a teacher? Like Cadence?"

Tatum considered this, taking in a deep breath and letting it out slowly enough to ponder the question. She frowned. "It wasn't on her bucket list. But, I mean, there's a lot of things I do that aren't on mine. Just natural things."

"I don't have one," Mila confessed.

Tatum looked at her. "A bucket list? Young people usually don't."

"You're young," Mila shot back.

"Well, I don't really have one. I just have one thing I

want to do. That's *it*."

"And if you do that one thing, your life will be complete? You can die happy?"

Tatum thought about it for a beat. Then two. "Does anyone really die happy?"

Mila got a funny look on her face, and it occurred to Tatum this could be the exact wrong thing to say.

She rushed to take it back. "Sorry I said that. I didn't mean it. I'm sure your dad was a happy man when he died." She tried for a smile and lifted her hand as if to offer the very house in which they sat as proof.

"Actually," Mila answered, her mouth odd angles, a cross between grief and reflection, "I like to think you're right. Who wants to die? My dad didn't. He was too happy. Too happy to die. But, I suppose, if you *can* be happy once death comes, he was." Her eyes glimmered and she swallowed past a budding tear.

Tatum gripped her knee and squeezed. "He'd want you to be a marine biologist, you know."

Mila blinked and wiped away the wetness, her eyes instantly clear. "What about your dad?"

Tatum stiffened. "My dad?"

"What would he want you to do?"

Her shoulders relaxed, and the answer came easily. "That's just the thing. You see, I wouldn't have a bucket list at *all*, actually. But now I do. Just the one thing. And, well, it was sort of *his* idea to begin with." She arched an eyebrow. "Want to know a secret?"

Mila leaned in and grinned like a little girl. "Yes."

"I'm patching things over with my sisters. I'm fixing it. That's my bucket list."

31

C adence set the shears down. They thudded on the tablecloth. She gave Darla a hard look. "A stereotype? You think that because I married an older man I became...a stereotype?" She gave her sister as blank a look as she could muster then folded her arms.

This would be good.

Darla let out a heavy breath. "Not a stereotype. That's not—" Then she searched the ceiling. "Actually, yeah. That's what I meant, Cade. A stereotype. Pretty young wife. Older, *richer* man. You never wanted marriage. Or kids. Then you signed on for the whole shebang." Darla met her gaze and held it. "Why?"

This was a slap in the face. A knife to the heart. "Hm, gee, Dar. Why do most people get married at all?" She held a hand to her mouth as if to prevent the slip that came next. "Oh, right. You seem a little confused on that point. Let me spell it out for you, dear." Cadence took pains to enunciate each and every word. "*Most* people marry for *love*. Not to fulfill some silly *list* they tote around like it's a set of directions on how to live life!"

Rage colored Darla's face red. But it changed on a dime, the color draining as fast as it had flushed up her neck and into her cheeks. "I'm gonna be sick," she managed before grabbing one of the orange buckets and retching.

Cadence watched in equal measures of horror and fascination. "You're not sick."

Darla looked up, running the back of her hand over her mouth before succumbing to a second brief round.

When she'd recovered and steadied herself at the edge of the table, Cadence grabbed her shoulder, her face softening. "Darla, are you—"

"Knock, knock!"

Cadence and Darla each swung her head toward the door.

Mason.

"Oh!" Cadence all but shouted as he stepped around the corner of the door.

Surprised, he glanced around.

"Sorry, I just—"

"Hello?" Lotte followed him in. "Mason was looking for something, and I thought we had one."

Satisfied that Cadence and Darla's conversation had remained private, she let out a breath and watched as Darla righted herself, her mouth a tight line. "What do you need?" Cadence asked, her tone as soft as she could make it.

Lotte held her palm up to him. "What did you say it was? Something for your boat?"

He cocked a half grin. "Yeah. It's an engine part. I, uh, well—I was hoping to see if maybe you had spares in your boatshed out back. I can take a look at yours, too. While I'm at it. Nothing much else to do until the party, so..." His lazy gaze turned on Darla. Cadence watched Darla look away.

Ashamed?

"Of course. Hendrik kept lots of spare parts there. You must know boat people."

"Well, not all service their own. I rarely do myself, but I don't know the folks here like I do in Birch Harbor. So." He shrugged.

After showing him out, Cadence returned to the back deck to find Lotte and her band setting up. It looked like a slow process. Cords and cables snaking treacherously across walkways. "Need anything?" she asked, hoping her implication hit. This was a mess. They needed to do better. Cadence narrowed her eyes on the particularly thick cord that ran directly into the back door.

"Duct tape would work," Lotte replied. "So no one trips."

Cadence clasped her hands. "You know there's an outlet here," she said, pointing just behind one of their speakers only to see it was already full. "Oh. Could you do a power strip? I think we'll want to keep the door closed. I already swatted one mosquito when I was in the shed."

"Early for mosquitos," Lotte grumbled back, "but yeah. That'll be way better."

Cadence went in search of a spare power strip, rummaging in the junk box of tech equipment left in

Hendrik's wake. He wasn't much for technology, but he'd had his gadgets. Police scanners, for fun. Radios for him and his friends on their boats. Old-man gizmos, she considered them. She pushed up the edge of her work shirt—Hendrik's. It was blue, not black. She was so close to some kind of end that she knew it was better to begin the transition. Her mourning couldn't go on forever.

Then again, how could Cadence possibly move on at all, what with Darla's continued accusations of scandal?

She found the power strip, passed it out to Lotte, and tracked down Darla, who'd been in the bathroom upstairs. Cadence's en suite, as she'd requested everyone use so as to preserve the cleanliness of the downstairs baths for guests.

"Darla." Her sister's face had regained its color. "Is that"—Cadence squinted—"fresh lipstick?"

"It's nothing."

"The party doesn't start for hours." Cadence cocked her head. "And Mason won't be back here until then."

"What are you suggesting?"

"You like him, but you've got a secret," Cadence accused as they stood in a valley between her chest of drawers on the right and nightstand on the left. What once felt like a too-small bedroom—what with all of Hendrik's Tommy Bahamas competing for space with Cadence's linen pants—now stretched in a wide yawn, engulfing the sisters like the Grand Canyon. An arid, dangerous zone of tragedy and...adventure?

Could it be that Cadence and Darla were on a journey? Like a pair of white-water rafters hiking down the treacherous switchbacks to the fertile river that waited below.

But what *really* awaited them? A standoff? A chance?

"I don't have a secret," Darla replied.

Cadence's eyes fell to Darla's hands. They lay across her lower abdomen, protectively. But when she looked again to Darla's face, it showed nothing short of terror. "Well," Cadence replied, offering a tentative smile, "you do now."

32

Cadence thought she had a clue about Darla's secrets, all of them. But she didn't, of course. Only Darla knew the truth. Her own complete history. Not even Tatum shared in it, either. The only other person who did have the full story was complicit, and *anyway*, that was old news. Even now, it was old news.

Handled.

Signed, sealed, and *served*.

What Cadence *thought* she knew wasn't anything, of course. It was a bug. A virus. A sticky travel sickness over-staying its welcome in Darla's body.

Then again, wasn't this on the list? Item number two?

Children.

The thought made her feel even sicker.

After leaving Cadence upstairs, Darla flew to her own bedroom in the next house. Mila and Tatum were at the breakfast bar so wrapped up in their own world they didn't see or hear her, but it was just as well.

Darla needed to be alone.

She had to process this. What Cadence thought. What Darla denied.

And, then, the truth.

The first thing she did, once tucked in the white caps of her bedding, was call Hunter.

He didn't answer.

She texted.

Need to talk. Important.

It worked, and he called, but the conversation went far differently than she'd imagined.

"Did you change your mind?" he asked before she'd even said hello.

"Change my mind?" Shaking her head, Darla pushed back up into a sitting position. "No."

"Then what's so important? Oh, wait. Let me guess. You left your Dutch oven at my house."

This was true, and Darla had seriously considered retrieving it once she was back in Detroit. But again. "No. Hunter, it's..." But as the words formed in her mind, she realized she had no proof. What if she *wasn't*? What if Cadence was wrong and *Darla* was right.

"What?" he was impatient. Always impatient.

"Actually, yes," she answered, swallowing hard. "The Dutch oven. I'd...well, I'm out of town now, but—" Oh, geez. He'd think she was covering up. *As if.* Darla cleared her throat. "Hunter"—her voice hardened—"I haven't taken a test, but—"

"Let me guess, Darla. You finally got what you wanted?"

A snort fell out of her mouth.

"Well, I am living on an island now," she answered. "So, technically, you're right."

He laughed. Short, derisive. "Yeah, well. If that's the case, you know how I feel."

She didn't. "What?"

"I was along for the ride as much as you were, Darla." Hunter squeezed the whole sentence onto one scornful sigh.

This was news to her. "What are you saying, Hunter?"

"I'm saying, if you're telling me what I think you're telling me, I want no part. I'll sign more paperwork if I have to. But you decided we were done. So we're *done*."

If cell phones had dial tones, she'd know for sure that he'd hung up. Instead, she sat in her bed, the phone frozen to her ear as she kept silent like a mouse. Listening hard. It was a joke. No way the man she'd planned to marry—the man she'd *almost* married and kind of actually *had* married—would do this. No *way*. Even Hunter.

SOMETIME LATER—AN hour? More?—Darla was rustled awake by the sound of her door opening and closing.

She peered, sleep dazed and dry mouthed, toward the source of the creaking wood. "Cadence?" Her sister's silhouette was unmistakable now.

Cadence lowered to the bed next to Darla's legs. A motherly sit, if there ever was one. In her clutches, a plain paper bag, the top rolled down clear to the bottom.

Darla sat up. "What time is it? Did I miss the reunion?"

"No." Cadence shook her head. "It's starting soon, though. I had Tatum come check on you. You've been asleep for hours." She chuckled. "Here."

Cadence passed the bag to Darla, who remained bleary and confused. "What's this?"

"Listen, Darla." Cadence kept her voice low and even. "I thought I never wanted children. But once Hendrik and I married, life changed for me. My priorities changed. Everything came into this sharp focus. I fell in love with the girls. With the island. Hendrik provided this life for me that I only ever saw in magazines at the Detroit Public Library." She laughed. Darla didn't, but she sat up straighter on the bed, feeling more awake now.

"Are you saying you *did* marry him for his money?"

Cadence cocked her head. "I married Hendrik because I fell in love with Mila first."

Darla's eyes grew wide, but Cadence just laughed.

"No. I mean, I figured whoever had raised this girl, *wow*. And then I met her sisters at some family event. And they impressed me, too. I wondered about their mother, but of course I soon learned that there was no mother. Not really. Then I met him." Cadence looked away, blinked, passed a hand beneath her eye. "And I saw the type of man who'd raised those three girls. Alone. He was different than Dad, but not better or worse. Whereas Dad didn't come from much and made things work, Hendrik came from a lot and made that work. Do you see what I mean?"

Darla shook her head.

"For all that he had here, Hendrik was down to earth. He liked to fish and read and spend time with his daughters. And friends. He was quiet but friendly. I loved him early and often, I like to say. We became best friends. In fact, for a while Hendrik was my only friend on the island." She paused and gave Darla a curious look. "I guess you don't know much about how our relationship progressed."

Again, Darla shook her head. Her mouth was dry to a breaking point, but she sat still, rapt. "No, not really. Back then, I was—" Where *was* Darla? What was she doing? "Starting my career." It was funny, how much Darla had thrown into teaching. Into theater. Both had only ever been passing interests. In fact, teaching wasn't even an interest. More of an obligation. An eventuality. Her mother had been a teacher. Cadence became one. So, Darla did, too.

"You were just starting your life, too," Cadence pointed out softly. "In our twenties, we're mostly figuring out who we are."

Darla stirred. "See, though. Cadence, that's where I've been coming from. When you met Hendrik you were what? Twenty-*seven*?"

"Something like that," Cadence answered with a smirk.

"You were too young to get caught up with an old man."

"Old*er* man," Cadence corrected. "Hendrik was barely fifty. Not old. Not by a long ways."

"Fair enough," Darla muttered. "Where are you going with this, though?" She pointed to the brown sack.

"Back then," Cadence continued, "I had every idea of

how my life would be. But that all changed. After we married, I told Hendrik I wanted kids. Kids of my own. I wanted them desperately."

Darla's eyes grew wide. "You *did*?" This wasn't the Cadence Darla knew. Then again, how long had it really been since she'd *known* her older sister? Over ten years now?

Cadence shook her head. "And he'd have given them to me. Every year for ten years, he wanted me to have whatever I wanted. And the thing was, whatever I wanted was usually the exact same thing that he wanted." A mirthless laugh slipped through her lips, rocking her backward. "Wow. It never felt like ten years."

That was it. That was the line. The line that changed Darla's heart. She'd been with Hunter for two years. And it had felt like twenty. "You loved him," Darla whispered.

Cadence's smile fell off her face like she'd been slapped. "With all of my being, I loved him. I still do." She dropped her head and Darla watched her hands squeeze the bag.

"Why didn't you have kids, then? I mean, with Hendrik?"

Cadence lifted her head, and the smile returned to her mouth. She handed the bag to Darla, who took it. "We tried."

Peeking into the bag, Darla's head snapped up. She felt confronted. With truth? With the future? With some twisted, joyful reality? "Where did you get this?"

Standing, Cadence smoothed her peach-colored dress. A lace-sheathed satin thing that Darla didn't recognize. "Like I said, for ten years, we tried." She winked and left.

Darla pulled the plastic-wrapped box from the bag and went straight to the bathroom.

33

After spending the morning piecing together whimsical flower arrangements—much to Cadence's chagrin—Tatum dashed back to her bedroom in the middle house to get ready.

The reunion meant relatively little to her. She had bigger and more important things to focus on. But seeing as it was Sunday, and the island slept on Sundays, her hands were tied well enough to resituate her focus on a little fun in the sun.

She tied a floral wrap across her abdomen, smudged coral-pink lipstick onto her pout, and returned to Cadence's house in search of Darla.

She ran into Mila first, who was heading upstairs to hide. "Have you seen Darla?"

"Um, I think Cadence went over to take her something, like, half an hour ago? Cadence is already back, so I'm guessing Darla should be over soon. The party starts in like five minutes. Mason is already here." Mila rolled her eyes.

Tatum left and looked for Mason. A hunch told her that if Darla *was* there, she'd be with him.

But she was wrong. "Where's Darla?" she whispered to Lotte, who was tuning a guitar. Lotte shrugged.

Fay was absent, predictably. Cadence appeared, tweaking place settings as Mason chatted up the rest of Lotte's band members. Some might find him annoying. He was always around, like he didn't have a life. Tatum thought he seemed nice enough, though.

"Cadence," Tatum hissed, "where's Darla?" Feeling uncomfortable was, well, uncomfortable to Tatum. Foreign. But here, in a new place with new people, it struck her that she was floating.

"She'll be over," Cadence answered, but her gaze turned to the back of the deck, toward the steps that led down to the boardwalk below. "Oh, geez." She propped her hands on her hips.

"Huh?" Tatum followed her sister's stare to see an unfamiliar man ascend the steps. "Oh, no. Early party guest?" She glanced at her phone. "Not *that* early."

"Not a party guest," Cadence shot back. "More like a party crasher." She raised her voice and called out across the expansive deck. "Rip! You can't be here."

Tatum watched with intense curiosity. *Rip?*

Mason crossed the deck and shook his hand. "What are you doing on this side of the lake?"

"Is Heirloom really a *side*? I take it more for the heart," Rip replied, a wry half grin on his dark stubble.

He locked eyes with Tatum, who hadn't realized she'd drifted to Cadence's side. Her curiosity had gotten the better of her, and her mouth was agape, too. She swallowed and matched his cocksure grin with one of her own. She immediately didn't like him. And that was saying something, because Tatum liked *everyone*.

"I very much disagree," Cadence answered, crossing her arms over her chest. "We're about to host an event here."

"Aha," he returned, "Hendrik would be proud."

Tatum watched as Cadence's pose softened. "What *are* you doing here, Rip?"

The dark-haired man gave her a look of confusion then twisted to Mason. "Mace said there was a party."

"Yeah, a family *reunion* party. Not a *party*!" Mason groaned and pushed his hand through his hair, but Tatum was too clever.

"Baloney. You two are like a pair of banger brothers." The insult came from nowhere. She rolled her eyes, too.

The men laughed, and Cadence joined them. "That sounds about right, if I know Rip." Then she did a double take at Tatum. "Oh, Tatum." She nodded to the party crasher. "Rip. Rip, this is my sister Tatum."

"I thought you looked familiar," he replied, stretching his hand for Tatum to take. Instead, though, she gave him a phony smile and just waved.

"We've never met." Unless...he'd attended Cadence's wedding? Tatum wasn't known for her sharp memory...

"True," he confessed, retracting his hand and pressing it to his chest, unaffected, it would appear, by her rejection. "I've seen your picture in the house." He dipped his head back so that his chin indicated the house behind her.

Oddly, Tatum felt unmoored by this stranger's familiarity with her new world. With Cadence's world.

She pressed her lips together and gave a short nod. "Oh."

"You came all the way here," Cadence said, tapping one foot on the wooden planks and humming after her thought. She threw up her hands. "Oh, heck. Just stay. You can help me. Come on." She waved him up, and just like that, the party grew by one.

Since Darla was still missing, Tatum felt itchy and bored. Especially once Cadence excused herself to welcome the trickle of guests.

Tatum wove through bouquets and white linen tables, her memory landing briefly on Cadence's wedding, so many years ago. Had Cadence found reminders, too, today? Or was she well enough distracted?

Pouring herself a glass of lemonade from the backup bottle in the fridge, she rejoined Lotte at the little bandstand. The band members behind her were playing their instruments, establishing a soft backdrop as new faces appeared up the backside of the property, from the lakeshore below. "What's your lineup tonight?" Tatum asked Lotte over the thrum of music.

"Some classics. Some of our stuff," Lotte answered, fiddling with her guitar again.

"I hope Cadence is paying you?" She raised an eyebrow.

"What?" Lotte called back as the bassist behind her turned up the volume. Lotte made a swirl with her finger at her ear. "I can't hear you!" She hooked her thumb behind her, to the rest of her group. "That's my cue!"

The music took off, and Lotte was right. An old party favorite.

Tatum would dance, if there were dancing, but for some reason she felt on edge. Maybe it was the fact that their big decision hung over her. They made the call, but they didn't have the framework in place to really commit. Despite Tatum's fly-by-the-seat-of-her-pants nature, she *did* want plans in place. Especially for her kids, who she missed to the point of homesickness, and Tatum had not expected to feel homesick on Heirloom Island. Not one bit.

"Dog owner?" came a voice behind her. Tatum jerked left to see it was the Rip character, who'd materialized out of thin air. "Sorry." He held his hands up. "I've been instructed to keep a lower profile."

"How do you know I'm a dog owner?" Tatum asked, settling back into her pensive position at the French double doors that led inside in case of emergency. *Still* no sign of Darla.

"Your shoulder." He pointed, his fingertip nearly touching the seam of her blouse—a bright red number that draped her body in a way that usually made Tatum feel *great*. So, why was she feeling annoyed?

She lifted her left shoulder to inspect it. A single fine dog hair. Two inches long. White and nearly imperceptible. It was a stretch for this guy to assume *dog hair*. Tatum brushed it off, certain that dog and cat fuzz had hopped a ride in her luggage, yes. But uncertain that she could tolerate standing next to this Rip person even a minute longer. "Could have been *my* hair," she retorted, looking with a purpose into the thickening crowd—well, not exactly *thick*, but thick enough that she could pretend she spotted someone important.

"No," he replied. "You're dark haired." Tatum's head swiveled toward him. "Like me," he added. "So, what do you have? A golden?"

Tatum laughed. "What kind of person has just *one*?"

To her great surprise, he deadpanned her. "The *worst* kind."

She looked at him anew, her eyes searching his face, dark stubble and hard lines—everything masculine that any other woman would fall head over heels for.

After mustering a smile, Tatum simply said, "Right," then walked away.

34

"Everything okay?" she whispered to Tatum, who'd appeared at her side as she stood at the top of the stairs, welcoming the last trickle of reunion guests up the stairs.

She'd known this would be a modest event, and so it had proved. Still, everyone dressed the part, in gauzy, summery whites and pastels or bright, beachy colors. Tanned shoulders and straw shoulder bags bobbed over the deck as family members, mostly all familiar with each other, hugged and cheek-kissed one another.

"Your friend, Rip, is annoying me," Tatum answered, glancing over her shoulder.

Cadence frowned and followed her gaze to where Rip stood awkwardly at the back doors. She returned her eyes to Tatum. "He's *family*," she pointed out as if it might mean something to Tatum.

But the answer only served to confuse her littlest sister. "I thought he *wasn't* part of the family."

"He's part of *my* family. Hendrik's youngest brother.

The girls' uncle." She jutted her chin toward Lotte and the band, the one representative of the three girls. It was fine that the other two tucked away inside. Better, probably, what with Tatum, Darla, and now Rip to manage. She didn't want the reunion guests to think Cadence and her own group were overtaking the evening events.

"Oh," Tatum replied. "Right."

"Have you seen Darla? She was supposed to be here by now."

"No," Tatum answered, "I was looking for her, too."

"I hope everything's okay." Cadence greeted what appeared to be the last couple and ushered them in.

Drinks and apps were staged impeccably on the outdoor bar for the Hannigans and the rest of their clan to help themselves to. They were set to mingle for the first half hour as Heir up There—Lotte's band—played on. After, Cadence, with help, would serve a light dinner. Dessert, coffee, and dancing or more mingling to follow. Since the Acton family, with the exception of Mason, was not attending, Cadence decided to downplay the reunion part, hoping no conflicts would arise among the tighter knit group and the outsiders.

The outsiders. Cadence kept a close watch. They were her more important guests in some way, but then again, important, too, were the Hannigans. One good recommendation from locals like them and Cadence could count on establishing herself quite handsomely as Heirloom Island's own events coordinator and *even* event locale.

Liesel, Mark, and Mason—the three outsiders of the bunch—blended as well as one might hope. The Hannigans swarmed Liesel, fascinated, it appeared, by either her Southern twang or foreign ways—small-town Indiana was different than Heirloom Island, even though it, too, was tiny.

Mason, affable and friendly, didn't even need Rip, who loitered like a sidekick by the doors. She ought to give him the boot, but then—

"There she is!" Tatum hissed.

The back doors cracked open and out slipped Darla. She wore a simple teal sundress, billowy and light. It set her brown eyes on fire, Cadence thought. "I need to check on her."

"I'll come," Tatum offered.

Cadence crossed the deck, weaving delicately between guests, until she stood in front of Darla. "Are you okay?"

Darla glanced from Cadence to Tatum and back again. "Did you tell her?"

Cadence's cheeks turned hot. "I wasn't sure there was something *to* tell," she replied, shifting her gaze to Tatum.

"Tell me what?" Tatum asked.

Cadence made a fast decision. Her eyes flew to Rip. "Hey. Can you sort of...cover for me? If anyone needs anything, just handle it?"

Rip pushed off the door, interlaced his fingers, and pressed them out in a stretch. "I'm on it."

∾

THE THREE OF them found themselves at the edge of the boardwalk, where the wooden slats disappeared into the grass-strewn sands of the Continental Coast.

Cadence stopped ahead of the other two and leveled her stare on Darla. "Well?"

Her lower lip trembled, and her hands shook as she lifted them to cover her face. Darla shook her head, her whisper muffled, but audible. "I'm pregnant."

35

S tunned, the trio had little choice other than to return to the party. Cadence promised she'd ensure the party ended on time.

Tatum walked Darla home, chatting excitedly the whole way.

Neither one bothered to linger to help with serving dinner or offer goodbyes to anyone. Not even Mason. Not even Rip. Darla was too anxious. Tatum too thrilled. This was a great irony, of course, since it was Darla who *wanted* kids and Tatum who guarded herself against the very notion of a human child. *Her* words.

Once back home, Darla's anxiety turned inward, twisting her stomach into knots. She wrapped herself in a flannel throw blanket and tucked into the crook of the sofa. "What do I do, Tate?" she asked her sister half miserably half coyly.

Despite the anxiety. Despite the circumstances, Hunter had been right.

This was *exactly* what Darla wanted. Just...not quite like *this*.

Tatum popped open Darla's laptop, her excitement bubbling to a breaking point. "Due date. If it's really Hunter's baby, then surely we can pin it down. Think, Darla."

"If it's really Hunter's baby?" Darla cried. "Who else's would she be? Or he? Geez, Tatum." Darla pursed her lips. She just wasn't the sort. Call her a prude. Call her old-fashioned. Darla didn't subscribe to the free sex movement. Far from it. Her sisters may not have realized as much, though. Since, by and large, they still didn't even know the full truth and nothing but the truth so help them.

"Okay, so...let me see here." Tatum tapped away at the keys, unaffected by the offense Darla took. "First day of your last cycle?"

Darla frowned, her eyebrows falling so heavily over her lashes she could feel the little black hairs poking up. Curse of long lashes, her mother would call it. Benefit, Cadence would call it. She thought another moment and came up empty. "It's been a while."

"A while?" Tatum looked alarmed. "A month? Two?" After Darla didn't answer. "*Three?*"

"Two. Probably two. I mean, I didn't notice, and...well..."

"We'll go back two months and use that date." Tatum tapped again then came up. "You're looking at the beginning of December. A winter baby!" she screamed, shoving the computer off her lap and lunging for Darla.

"Careful!" Darla cried back. "Careful! I'm in a delicate condition."

Tatum took a breath and let it out, content as could be. "Wow. Okay. So, does this change things?"

"Change what things?" Darla asked, hugging her knees to her chest. Of course it changed things. It changed her life. She'd be doing this alone. This motherhood thing. Without Hunter, for one. And now— "Do mean, like, with us staying on the island?"

"What do you mean staying on the island?"

Cadence had appeared in the back doorway. She wore the same party dress as earlier, but slung over one shoulder was a canvas tote.

"Isn't the party still going?" Darla asked.

"Yes. For another hour," Cadence answered. "But—" She smiled. "This seems more important."

Darla felt suddenly emotional. For the first time, in fact, she was emotional. More emotional than a teardrop here or there. The sort of emotional that welled deep inside, threatening to cave your chest in on your heart and cause serious, hospital-worthy damage. She sucked in a deep breath, managing one more question. "Who'll handle things over there?" Her voice cracked, and Cadence rushed in, squeezing between Tatum and Darla on the sofa.

She ran the back of her hand along Darla's cheek. Something Mom would have done. "I've got enough helpers over there to run the America's Cup, if I wanted. But even the America's Cup couldn't compare to news of the first Sageberry sister's baby."

Said like that, the truth raged through Darla's body like a flood. The gates burst, and she did, too.

"What am I going to do?" she sobbed against Cadence's shoulder.

"You'll do what countless women before you have done," Cadence answered quietly. "You'll be a mother."

36

The following week was as much a blur as the first few days. Darla slept in as late as she could stand to, regaining some of the rest she'd lost Sunday night and then Monday and Tuesday.

Hunter didn't take her calls, but that was just as well. He'd given her the information she needed.

Tatum had scored an interview with Island Koken. "Just in the meantime," she'd insisted.

Her long-term goal was to scour the island for the perfect stretch of land on which to erect a new county animal shelter. Cadence had tried to convince Tatum that Heirloom wasn't the place for a county facility. It'd be too hard to boat animals in.

That's when Mason had chimed in.

It was Friday, and the women plus Mason were enjoying lunch on Cadence's back deck. Up the boardwalk, Liesel and Mark and their family were packing to check out.

"What about an animal ferry?" Mason suggested. "I

mean, look at the *Birch Bell*, it's a ferry for humans. You could send an animal ferry to the mainland when you have a transfer coming in."

Darla couldn't help but throw in her two cents. "Sounds like a big extra expense. As it is, you'll have to beg for money running a nonprofit," she pointed out.

"It's not much of an extra expense if you already have a boat," Mason responded.

Since Darla had become aware of her condition—which she'd only shared with Hunter and her sisters—she'd folded into herself. Not in a bad way, though. In a responsible way.

Pregnancy and a baby—it had been at the top of Darla's list for so long that she'd dared not do a thing to jeopardize it. Even if circumstances were less than ideal, for Darla, this was *it*. She'd do whatever it took to make things work.

Initially, her gut reaction had been to run home. But as the week rolled on and she watched Cadence settle in with the girls and Tatum turn giddy over her interview and a chance at a new start...Darla wondered what there was to run home *to*. She had no apartment. Her gig at the university was as evanescent as her vacation on Heirloom. Why not uphold the pact she'd made with Tatum?

So, for lunch that day, she and Tatum had decided to move forward with their proposal. Mason's joining them felt like an obstacle, though. Especially now. Their flirtation dead in the water, Darla turned awkward in his presence.

She could tell he could tell something had changed.

"I have a boat," Cadence said, glomming on to Mason's idea about the animal ferry.

Tatum appeared to mull the idea over. "It's sort of... small, though. But choosers can't be beggars."

Darla laughed and shook her head, catching Mason's eyes on her. She looked away. "It's beggars can't be *choosers*, Tate."

Shrugging, Tatum was eager to take any suggestion and run with it. "Mason's right." Then she frowned. "Maybe someone around the island has a bigger boat? Something like a houseboat. Something I can rent for when I need to taxi out and in?"

Mason snapped his fingers. "You know who has a houseboat," he replied. "Rip."

Mason was new to the area. Six months in and already well acquainted with locals, apparently. "You're sure?"

"Sure as I am eating turkey sandwiches with you fine ladies. I should know," he added. "I live on it."

37

Dead silence pooled across the table, descending like heat. It was broken only when a cool breeze, like magic, curled over them. "You live on a boat?" Tatum's question was meant to be innocent, but she could see it struck the wrong note.

She'd missed something her sisters had not.

But Mason, like Tatum, appeared blissfully unaware. "Yeah, sure. I rent it from Rip. So, once I leave here, I'll post up north of Birch Harbor, where he's got a private dock. Seems like everyone and their mother have a private dock on Lake Huron." Shrugging, he took a generous bite of his sandwich.

"And you think Rip would lend it out to me?"

"If he doesn't sell it first. That's why I'm renting. He needs the extra cash. Not all Van Dams are loaded."

Tatum felt Cadence ice over. This was not how she wanted today to go. She had her interview that afternoon. Only good vibes could get her through it and to the point where she and Darla sprung their grand plan on

Cadence. "Who's loaded?" Tatum laughed nervously. "No one in this neck of the woods, that's for sure."

Cadence crossed her arms. "Rip and Hendrik went rounds after their father's passing. That was a long time ago, but I know Rip still thinks Hendrik won and he lost."

Mason held up his hands. "Didn't mean to make accusations. Sorry. I should have watched my words."

Darla interjected. "Cadence has to go back to teaching. Hendrik's healthcare costs crippled them. In fact, she'd lose the houses if she didn't rent them out. No reason for her to bear extra expenses nowadays."

Tatum tried to catch Darla's eye. Wasn't this the moment? They could pitch it—their great idea?

But Darla wouldn't look at her.

"How big is St. Mary's?" Mason asked. "Do they have openings from year to year?" His tone carried a suggestion, an implication, that Tatum didn't follow. But she *did* notice Darla twitch. Her eyes widened and she leaned forward, willing Darla to meet her gaze.

"They don't have high turnover, and I'm not qualified for the openings they currently have—I was a math teacher. But I know the principal. He'll bring me on board if I ask. Soon, that is."

"Do you really have to teach *and* rent out the houses?" Tatum asked, genuinely curious. "I mean, based on what *we* paid, and what I know Liesel and her family paid, it seems like you'd be covered. You don't have a mortgage. And then what about the girls? Could they help?"

"If I didn't have to depend on vacation rentals, then maybe I wouldn't have to teach."

"Don't you *want* to teach?" Darla asked, apparently dumbfounded.

Tatum smirked. Darla sounded like Mom. Darla *was* Mom. In so many ways.

Cadence let out a sigh. "I don't know *what* I want. I want...I want to live. I want to do new things. Get my mind clear." She shook her head as if she was literally clearing her mind, then smiled. "Does that make sense?"

"I don't know what I'd do if I didn't teach," Darla said. "It's...what I do."

"You don't love it, though," Tatum pointed out. "I mean, you don't seem to *love* it."

"I'm not the sort who needs to love my career. Or even my job. I'm the sort who *needs* it."

This made little sense to Tatum, at least at first.

Soon enough, though, she scratched meaning from it. Slowly at first, then it hit her like a ton of bricks. Darla *was* Mom. Not because they were both teachers. Not like Cadence, who'd loved teaching until she met a different love. A true love. Darla was Mom in that she needed a purpose. A way to support herself. She'd needed it when she was with Hunter. And she'd need it in order to stay on the island. "What position is open at St. Mary's?"

Cadence scrunched her mouth into a tight knot. "Hm." She thought for a minute, her blinking eyes narrowing on the pitcher of lemonade that sat sweating at the center of the table. Another breeze cut through them, lifting tendrils of Tatum's hair and cooling her neck like a silk scarf. She had to stay. Cadence's answer *had* to be the right one.

Cadence frowned at last. "English. Junior high English."

English wasn't theater, but Tatum had a feeling she could make it be. "English, like Shakespeare?"

Cadence gave a shrug. "I guess?"

Tatum stared hard at Darla, giving her an urgent look and a lift of the eyebrows.

When Darla still said nothing and Cadence still didn't catch on and Mason still continued to munch noisily on his sandwich, Tatum decided she had to say it. It had to be said, and she had to be the one to say it. "Darla and I are going to stay on the island. We're going to rent the middle house from you, Cadence. And Darla needs to get a job."

Cadence's face opened in shock, but Tatum saw Darla remain as still as a statue.

"At least," Tatum went on, "until the baby comes."

That's when everything fell well and truly apart. Darla's stillness broke, and she cried. Cadence chastised Tatum like she was their mother. So then Tatum cried. Because Darla and Tatum were crying and for every other reason in the book, Cadence cried, too.

Mason was the only one who remained calm. *Clueless* may have been a better word, Tatum realized. "What baby?" he asked.

All three women turned to him, open mouthed and tear streaked.

Tatum tried to discreetly glance at Darla, wondering if she'd fess up.

But Cadence broke the silence first.

"The newest Sageberry baby, of course. *Our* baby."

38

C adence didn't know if Darla wanted to tell Mason. Or if it mattered. But she knew what it was to have hard news like that. Undeliverable news. The kind she'd had to give her very own sisters and mother less than a year earlier.

The next day, after Mason had returned to his houseboat on the Birch Harbor side of the lake, and after Tatum had nailed her interview with the Koken, Cadence found a moment to steal Darla.

"Want to take a walk on the beach?" she asked as the two leaned into opposite sides of the doorway at the middle house. The house where Darla was supposed to have left by now. The house that Tatum insisted they'd rent. It all seemed like such a long shot. Like a pipe dream, for all three of the sisters. Especially for Cadence, who'd do whatever it took to get them to stay. She just needed to find a way to say that. After all, a week earlier, she'd effectively given them the boot. Now here they all were, changed.

Darla agreed and let her in. It was faster to cut through the house and down the back stairs.

Once at the edge of the water, below the boardwalk and yards off from the trio of Van Dam houses, Cadence spoke first. "When you called and told me Dad was in the hospital, I was here."

A shadow crossed Darla's face and she slowed. "What do you mean *here*? I know you were here. I mean, I figured you'd be home."

"No, I was walking here. By the water. It was the first break I'd had from holding vigil at Hendrik's bedside. In *days*. For days, Darla, I'd tended to his every last need. And I was happy to. I loved that I could do that for Hendrik, and I don't regret it."

Confusion washed over Darla's face.

"I took a break, and I came out here, and you called and told me that it was time. That he was going. In a day or maybe two days. You didn't say I had a decision to make. Maybe I didn't tell you, because I didn't realize it was a decision. Not yet." Cadence looked up at her own house, which they now stood behind. She wrapped her arms across her body, hugging herself against the chill of the fall of night. It was past seven, and the early summer heat was no match for evening on the lake.

"What are you talking about, Cadence?" Darla had wrapped her arms around herself, too.

"I told you I'd be there. That I'd drive like the wind and be there," Cadence told her.

Darla's expression was unreadable, so Cadence pressed on. "But when I went back in, Hendrik flatlined. That's when he slipped into the coma." Cadence swallowed hard and blinked away wetness. "While I was out here. Walking. Taking a *break*. Talking to *you*."

Her face broke, and Darla grabbed Cadence's arm, tugging it free.

The sisters held each other for a long time. So long, that once they pulled away, their faces were wet, but they were no longer sobbing.

Darla spoke first. "I didn't want you to pick Dad over Hendrik," she said, her voice still trembly.

Cadence pressed her mouth into a line. "If you did, I understand why. But I want you to know that my marriage to Hendrik wasn't a scandal." She paused a beat. "Or a stereotype. Just because we didn't fit some perfect image of husband and wife doesn't mean we weren't head over heels for each other. I loved him, Darla."

"I know that now," Darla whispered back. Her eyes twinkled, and Cadence knew there was more there. More to say. She could talk about her regret. How she hadn't walked the lake until that very moment. She could talk about how she had wanted to leave Heirloom and never look back. How she'd wanted everything and everyone to *go away*. Until Tatum and Darla had turned up on her doorstep.

Instead, she figured it was a good time to offer her little sister a nugget of wisdom. Widow wisdom. Big sister wisdom. The sort of wisdom that came only from a life of regrets and wrong decisions and good decisions and things that shouldn't be regrettable but, still, were. Unavoidably regrettable. "It's okay to do things for yourself, Darla. Now that you're going to be a mother, I think you should know that."

"Being a mother is a selfless thing," Darla answered.

"So is taking care of a dying husband. But even though I would take back that walk if I could—I would be at Hendrik's side if I could—I needed it. The time for me. The moment to myself."

Darla's chest heaved a sigh. "I have lots of that now. Especially with no job."

"I can get you a teaching job at St. Mary's. If that's what you want. But I'm not talking about work."

"What are you talking about, then? Sister time? Trust me, I know when to establish boundaries with you and Tatum." She smirked then laughed, and Cadence laughed, too.

The laughter died fast. "I'm talking about love."

Darla laughed again. A loud, fake laugh. "Love, hah! I already tried that."

"It's at the top of your bucket list, right? Tatum told me." Cadence eyed her.

"Marriage is at the top. And, like I said, been there, tried that. Didn't work. Onto the next thing."

"You didn't try it, though," Cadence argued. They were walking up to her back deck now, where a heat lamp stood, tempting them toward it.

"Of course I did. With Hunter. He's ready to sign away parental rights and everything." She made a *tsk* sound. "See? Didn't work."

"You tried a boyfriend. A fiancé. Planning a wedding. You didn't try marriage, though. It's different." Cadence said this having done all those things. Being all those things.

But Darla stopped dead in her tracks at the top of the stairs at the edge of the deck. "Actually, I did."

"Huh?" Cadence squinted at her through the darkness. "What are you talking about?"

Darla held up her right hand and tugged loose a white gold band. One that had sat innocuously on her right pinky finger the duration of her time on Heirloom. "Hunter and I. Technically, we're married."

39

Darla was surprised to see that Cadence *was not*. She was so unaffected that Darla wanted to cry all over again.

But that was probably the hormones.

Cadence simply asked, "Did you elope?"

Sadly, no. Darla and Hunter were far from eloping. Eloping was romantic. They did the opposite. Having been afraid that things would get crazy closer to the wedding, Darla had dragged him to the courthouse where they had an official give them sterile legalese for vows as a secretary and courier looked on as witnesses. It was the smart thing, she'd told Hunter. That way, they could have their pretty garden ceremony and do all the fluff and not worry about signing anything or mailing anything or going to the courthouse later when the post didn't make it. Whatever. She wanted to be ahead.

Now, she felt behind.

And now, Hunter still hadn't signed the papers. And he had made no indication that he would. What was worse was that she didn't have a reliable address to give him. So, just the day before she'd texted him Cadence's. On the off chance she really would stay—that she would apply at St. Mary's and teach Shakespeare to preteens and have lunch dates with Mason...

But then visions of the baby materialized in her head, and she wondered why she hadn't already hightailed it home. Home to where her doctor lived and her mother lived and her life had been...well...forever. Home to where Hunter was, too.

Not that she loved him. She didn't. That was the issue. And it was too bad, too. Loving him would have been easier. She'd have assumed he loved her, too, and together they would love their baby. They *would*.

But here was Darla, on an island hundreds of miles away. Pretending that bucket lists were more important than things like ob-gyns and home loans and his-and-her hand towels.

After explaining everything to Cadence, they both opted to give up on the night. Too much hard stuff. Heavy stuff. They'd meet again the next morning.

Saturday. They'd talk about the future, and Cadence promised to grant a few more pearls, and Darla promised to at least pretend that she didn't already know everything.

Hah.

Now it was Saturday morning, and she was due at Cadence's for breakfast. Tatum was already off, heading excitedly to her training at the Koken. The three girls weren't around, either. They'd each managed to pick up things to do now that summer was in full swing.

Boyfriends or jobs or hobbies—summer business. The sort Darla now found herself craving in the absence of, well, everything else in life.

She made her way out across the deck and over to Cadence's, preferring the longer trek that was the back way now. In her head, she rehearsed what Tatum had told her to say. What if they rented the house? What if she applied at St. Mary's? Would Cadence be able to help with the baby? Would this baby really become what Cadence had told Mason? A Sageberry baby?

A boat motor blurred her concentration, and Darla looked off to the lake.

It was coming straight for the Van Dam dock at the backside of Cadence's house.

Driving it was Mason.

He waved at her.

Darla's heart sank, and the nausea from earlier she'd thought she'd quelled roared instantly back to life, nearly doubling her over. She swallowed it down and tried to focus on the fresh air. The cool morning breeze. Anything other than Mason Acton.

"Ahoy!" he hollered, hopping out and jogging straight for Darla.

She wanted desperately to disappear beneath the planks of the boardwalk, but it was too late. "Hi," she mustered, pressing her hand against her torso out of a new habit. She thought she saw his eyes dip to where her hand rested. Oh, well.

"I tried to call ahead and give you a warning only to realize I don't have your number."

She squinted. "A warning?"

"I left my wallet in the house. Been looking for it everywhere."

Darla suppressed a snort. Sure. Then, she grinned and said it aloud. "Sure."

He returned her smirkish smile and gestured back toward the middle house. "May I?"

"Go for it. I'm just joining Cadence for breakfast." Even as the words slipped through her lips, she knew she grimaced. "Want to join us?"

It was supposed to be just Cadence and Darla. They were going to call her principal and see about that English position. They were going to enjoy each other's company fully and truly for the first time during Darla's visit.

Now, there was an interloper to consider.

But he passed her, heading toward the middle house, and waved her off. "I don't want to overstay my welcome."

Something churned in Darla's stomach. "Mason, wait." It was ridiculous. Humiliating that she felt this way. Totally inappropriate and wildly indecent. Mixed emotions tumbled around in her brain until the smart thing took hold. "I can't give you my number," she said.

He stopped, and his smile slipped away. In its place... something unreadable. "Because you're pregnant?"

Her face went sheet white. He'd pieced everything together. Cadence's sly explanation wasn't sly enough. Darla took a step back. "That's not what—I'm not, like, *suggesting* anything." She took a second step back.

He matched her step with one of his own. Toward her. "Pregnant women can have friends."

Darla pursed her lips. "I know that."

Mason cocked his head. "We can be friends."

"I'll be busy. Trying to get a job here. Among everything else in my life." She smoothed her tunic down her torso. Soon, she'd be shopping for maternity clothes. Something she ought to be doing in the comfort of her hometown with her husband and—

"Yeah," Mason answered, scratching the back of his head. "I'm pretty busy, too."

"And anyway," Darla replied, "you live across the lake."

"True. On a boat. You'd just throw up all the time. If we ever hung out, I mean."

Darla nodded urgently. "Right." She licked her lips. "Anyway, the back door's unlocked." She lifted her hand back toward his destination. The house they'd shared for a week. Where everything started so flirtatiously. Where she might have had a rebound. A new beginning. Where she still had a new beginning, only of a different brand.

"Maybe I'll see you around the lake, Darla," Mason said, giving her a sad smile and a half wave before shoving his hands into his jeans pockets and striding off hurriedly.

Darla chewed the inside of her cheek and turned back toward Cadence's house.

"Darla!"

She spun around.

Mason had jogged back, closing their gap to just a few feet. "If you ever need anything. Anything at all." Then his Adam's apple bobbed, and his gaze fell again to her belly. "I've had a little experience with pregnant women."

"You have kids?" she asked, awed by the fact that she

didn't know that. That they'd spent a week together, and she didn't know that.

"No," he answered abruptly, giving her a sad look. "But I almost did."

He turned and jogged back, and it occurred to Darla that even if she didn't want his help, she couldn't exactly call him now. Now that she'd cut their potential friendship off at the pass.

Her stomach churned and she backed away, twisting to the last boardwalk house. Cadence.

Once there, she found Cadence setting their lunch table on the deck. "Hey."

Cadence glanced up, a smile pricking the corners of her mouth. "He's a nice guy."

"You were watching us?" Darla lowered into a seat, suddenly exhausted.

Cadence ignored the question. "Did he say he left his wallet?"

"Yeah." Darla looked across the decks to catch Mason leaving. Leaving the house. Leaving nothing behind save for fleeting, meaningless memories Darla would turn to for warmth. Comfort. Hope, maybe.

"Rip told me all about him, you know."

Darla studied Cadence, expectant. "And?"

"His wife had a miscarriage. Late term. It broke them. Well, according to Rip, not *him*. But her. She ended the marriage, left him heartbroken, I guess. Took him a while to get over it, and Rip says they connected through some ancestry thing. I guess Mason wanted to go back to his roots. Figure things out."

Darla frowned, angry on Mason's behalf. Sympathetic for his wife. Sad for both of them.

"Listen, Darla," Cadence said, sitting across from her, "I know now isn't the time. In fact, maybe there will never be a time, but once things are settled and you've got your job." Cadence simpered. "Once Tatum has her kids back here, and you've all settled the living arrangements—"

Darla laughed.

"Anyway, after you find your new normal, Darla, you should go back to your bucket list."

"Pfft." Darla rolled her eyes half-heartedly. "It's too late for that."

"Darla"—Cadence lowered her chin and gave her sister a hard look—"get your divorce squared away. Serve Hunter. Get a job. Have your baby and raise her. And just remember, it's never too late for love."

EPILOGUE

Fall cut a sharp contrast to summer on Lake Huron. Cool evenings became cold nights, and long days became, well, normal in length.

The three sisters had found a new stability in life.

Cadence did return to the classroom. She hoped one day she'd have the pleasure of teaching her grandchildren—future generations of Van Dams. Of course, they wouldn't be Van Dams. The girls would marry off. Lotte was already on track. Come late July, she had moved to Nashville, alone. There, she'd carved out a new life for herself with a new band. New name. New hope, as she'd told Cadence on the phone.

Fay had moved out of the boardwalk house, finding it too difficult to concentrate on her writing with *people* around. She rented a loft space in a back barn of an orchard just outside of Birch Harbor. She worked days at the orchard and its adjoining bakery. Early mornings and late nights, she spent toiling at her laptop. Working on the next great American novel, she'd told Cadence.

When Cadence asked where Fay had derived any struggle—anything from which to tug loose that kind of inspiration one needed for such an undertaking, Fay's response was a surprise. "I want to find my mother."

It was just after six, and phone calls with Fay had grown pleasantly common at that early hour. Cadence had made a habit of taking her coffee on the back deck in the autumn mornings, wrapped in a flannel blanket and tucked into the crook of her chaise longue, her cell phone on speaker as she sipped from a porcelain mug and listened with curiosity. "You mean you're using your mom for inspiration? For a fictional story? For a novel?"

Fay sighed heavily on the line. "Cadence, you're our mom, first of all. But that's my struggle. Even through my luck of having you, it's the missing piece in my life."

"Of course it is," Cadence responded, delicate and tentative. "So, is this more of a memoir?"

"No. Nothing like that. Just a way to understand women who give up motherhood. It's the story of a woman who leaves her family to be happy, but she never does find it. Even when she leaves and does the thing she thinks will solve her troubles, there's a hole."

"It's your way of gaining closure. And," Cadence suggested, "maybe some retribution?"

"It's my way of understanding her," Fay replied.

"But if you know how the story ends—with her continued emptiness—then are you actually seeking to understand? Or seeking to fulfill your own need? That need to explain the inexplicable?" Cadence was no philosopher and even less a therapist. But she *was*, well, a mom, as Fay had put it.

"I'm...well...I guess I'm looking for—"

"Fay," Cadence said, her voice low, soft, "it's okay, you know."

"What? What do you mean?"

Cadence cleared her throat. "If you're looking for your mom—for Katarina—it's okay. I would, too. If I were you."

"You would?" Fay asked.

"And if it's writing a book that takes you on that search, then all the better."

Cadence could hear Fay let out a breath on the other end of the line. "Thanks, Cadence," she said. "I hope you know this doesn't mean I think of you as anything different. You'll always be my mom."

"And you'll always be my daughter. You and your sisters." Cadence beamed for the middle child. The dark, quiet one. The introspective one who now lived in that little loft at the orchard across the lake. "Come home sometime, okay, Fay?"

"Okay. *Mom*."

The word made Cadence break, but she held it together long enough to end the call and brace herself against the railing of the deck. There, she breathed in the smell of the lake. She thought of Hendrik. Of her sisters. Of her *daughters*. And of what the future held for her there, at her home on the boardwalk.

AFTER TURNING down the next year's contract with the university, Darla accepted a smaller position, closer to *home*. She'd be teaching English, with a focus on Shakespeare and drama, to seventh and eighth graders at St. Mary's of the Isle Catholic School.

This job would be a departure for Darla. Not only from the age group she normally worked with but also because of the content. Still, it was a reminder that Darla only ever taught theater because it was what she *did*. Where her passion lay? That remained to be seen.

Moving to Heirloom Island had turned out to be more than a bucket-list-worthy dream vacation. Island life could be real life. She'd also come to figure out exactly why people in little tourist towns slung the word *local* around like a badge of honor. Living among people who *summered* there or *popped over for a day trip* demanded a different sort of patience than big-city folk would ever appreciate.

It wasn't only island living, however, that extended beyond that ten-point to-do list. Halfway through her pregnancy, healthy and on track, Darla realized some goals in life weren't just checklist items. With her divorce firmly secured and her housing arrangement set—she and Tatum rented the middle house from Cadence, naturally—stability felt close. But still just out of reach. Part of that may have been Tatum and her flock of furry pets overrunning the house day and night. That middle property felt less like Darla's and more like the shelter that Tatum was so desperate to open.

Then again, perhaps working played into Darla's sense of moorlessness. Her own mother had stayed home when the girls were young, tending to them night and day. Who would tend the Baby Sageberry?

Tatum offered. She worked mostly evenings and weekends. And Cadence said Mila was interested in babysitting. She needed to save up for her transfer to Wayne State, after all, where she would study biology eventually. After that, the youngest Van Dam girl wanted to attend grad school on the Atlantic Ocean. New England, ideally.

Those loose plans helped get Darla through the wakeful nights of those middle months of pregnancy.

She saw a life for herself beyond this particularly challenging transition. She did. She saw a family life. One with her sisters, yes. But another, too. Maybe, one day, a strong man. Of the sort who wouldn't mind stepping into fatherhood less than naturally.

It was Cadence who assured Darla that they were out there. "Those types who didn't see parenting for themselves until they were in love with a parent. People like me," she'd said.

This gave Darla hope.

And sometimes, when she was too restless to watch reality TV with Tatum and too irritable to chat on the deck with Cadence, Darla would walk the lake, no matter how cool a night it was. She'd walk and she'd imagine Mason Acton's boat. The one she knew. The one she could only picture. Just miles away, on the adjacent shores of Birch Harbor. She pictured him teaching at the school there. Singing high and low with choir types. Types that ran parallel to theater types. She pictured his past—the wife and the baby that never was—and Darla wondered what regrets he had. And if they were very different from hers. The sort of regrets that really weren't quite regrets. But, rather, were those pieces in life that didn't exactly feel like decisions. Those pieces in life that *were not* decisions. Fate. Fate that you couldn't go taking back. And that you wouldn't, probably, anyway.

Darla finished one such walk, feeling particularly wired. She climbed the stairs of the back deck and slipped inside, hankering for a cup of hot cocoa.

Quitting coffee had been one of the hardest parts of pregnancy, ridiculously. It was only that evening, a very chilly one, at the beginning of October that it occurred to her she might find a good substitute. Now that autumn had descended over the island, hot cocoa just felt right.

Tatum reclined on the sofa, two of her dogs snoring on her lap, and her cat curled around her head as something silly played out on TV.

"Want a drink?" Darla called as she rummaged in the cupboard for two suitable mugs, waiting for Tatum's answer.

"No thanks," Tatum replied and pushed the animals off so she could stand and join Darla in the kitchen. "I went for a bike ride earlier today. Almost made it across the entire island."

"Wow," Darla replied admiringly. "I need to do a little more exercise. I've heard postpartum it only gets harder."

"You'll be one of those mystery moms who comes out looking like you were just hiding a basketball under your shirt the whole time." Tatum grabbed a chocolate from the bowl on the bar. Darla's most recent installation to the house. "Anyway, I saw a sign for a property for sale, but I had Angus with me, and I got nervous he was too tired to go any farther."

"What's the property?" Darla asked, studying a mish-mash of glasses and aluminum tumblers. None of which was quite right for hot cocoa.

"I couldn't tell. It's a place at the far south end of the island, I think. For sale by owner thing. There were wooden boards with red spray paint pointing on and on, and I finally gave up. I'm going to go back tomorrow."

"That's exciting," Darla acknowledged. "Let me know if you want company."

Tatum yawned and nodded, then indicated she was off to bed. "It's Saturday. I work morning shift. Meet me here after? We'll go together?"

"Sure." Darla smiled her sister off and watched the parade of pets follow Tatum upstairs.

She returned to her quest, her gaze landing on a distinctly unfamiliar porcelain mug hiding in the back corner of the cupboard. Had she been drinking coffee all these months, she'd have seen it. But she wasn't, so...

Darla stood on her tiptoes and managed to hook it with her finger and slide it out from its nest of drinking cups.

When she did, a piece of paper fluttered from the mug, landing squarely in front of her.

On it, ten digits. A phone number. Local, by the area code. No name. Beneath the number, the words *No rush*.

Darla blinked at the paper for a moment, only to come to the conclusion it must have been a leftover of one of the girls. Lotte, Fay, or Mila. Maybe even an old Van Dam, from decades ago. Though the little piece was bright white. The numbers crisp. No yellowing. No dust.

Thinking little more on it, Darla pressed a finger into

the center of the digits and pushed the small paper across the bar to the chocolate dish, pinning it there for future investigation.

She blew into the porcelain chamber, clearing any dust that might have lingered, though there was none. Then she took it to the sink to rinse.

Only when she finally turned the mug over in her hands, running it beneath the warm water, did she finally see the engraving. *Just Leave Me the Heck Alone While I Figure Out My Life.*

Darla's other hand flew to her mouth.

Mason.

Her throat clenched at the silly memory.

And her heart swelled at what, someday, may be.

THE NEXT MORNING, Tatum awoke with a good feeling. So good a feeling, in fact, that she left the house early, opting to drive out to the property before beginning her shift.

It was early. Too early. That didn't matter, though. All she needed was to get a sense of if the land for sale could comfortably house a good-sized building. If there were flat spots for dog runs and if there were any buildings on the property. A house would be okay. An outbuilding would be better. All she needed in order to get started were four walls. The rest could come with time.

She drove out past the wooden signs with their red spray paint, driving until she was certain she was about to roll into Lake Huron.

Then she came upon it.

The property was more than just land—and lots of it. About a quarter mile up the dirt drive she found an old farmhouse, which was funny to Tatum. An island farm? Made no sense.

Then again, she knew that the area was established in the early 1900s. Surely, they had farms about.

Uncertain if the house was inhabited but too excited to be careful, Tatum parked and jumped out of her car. She walked up to the place to see that the building was as abandoned as could be. Broken windows, some boarded up, some not. Rotted siding and peeling paint. A mess, is what it was.

She started around the house, and by the time she came to the back of it, a second structure came into view. Something between a barn and a shed. Big, but...primitive in shape.

A frigid breeze cut across Tatum's face. In Michigan, fall bled quickly into winter. Especially out on the water, where the moisture added to an ongoing chill. Christmas would come soon. And at Christmastime, while everyone else was thinking about great big fir trees and Black Friday and when to thaw the turkey, Tatum was thinking about the animals. The ones who didn't make the cut as Christmas gifts. The ones who'd never known a warm home. Cold. Lonely.

She wandered into the open-faced shelter. In the center of it stood a shabby wooden trough. Old-fashioned looking. A feeding crib for horses, maybe. Way back when. A crib that had once held hay, maybe.

It reminded Tatum of something, though she couldn't

put her finger on it. No matter. She took out her phone and dialed the number from the final wooden sign.

It would be Thanksgiving before she'd pull together the loan. Pull together the meager down payment. Convince Cadence to cosign and Darla that the project wouldn't interfere with the baby.

But by then, Tatum would come to own that property with the tumble-down farmhouse in front and the old open-air barn out back. The shelter with its crib for hay. Hay for the animals.

By then, Tatum would have the very beginnings of Heirloom Island's first and only animal shelter.

CONTINUE THE SAGA. Order *The Manger House* today.

Looking for more? Try *Harbor Hills*, another heart-warming saga. You can learn more at elizabethbromke.com.

ALSO BY ELIZABETH BROMKE

Heirloom Island:

The Manger House

Hickory Grove:

The Schoolhouse

The Christmas House

The Farmhouse

The Innkeeper's House

The Quilting House

Harbor Hills:

The House on Apple Hill Lane

The House with the Blue Front Door

The House Around the Corner

The House that Christmas Made

ABOUT THE AUTHOR

Elizabeth Bromke is the *USA Today* bestselling author of over a dozen women's fiction and romance titles.

Liz and her husband and son live in northern Arizona. There, they spend time together reading, taking walks with their sweet pup, Winnie, and working on puzzles.

Stay in touch with the author by joining her newsletter at elizabethbromke.com or searching for her on Facebook, Instagram, Twitter, and Pinterest. Liz would *love* to hear from you!

ACKNOWLEDGMENTS

A huge thanks to my fabulous editing team: Beth Attwood, Lisa Lee, Elise Griffin, and Krissy Moran. Thank you so much for fine-tuning this book! I am a better writer thanks to you three!

Stephanie Irwin, thank you for becoming a source of critical support for Ed and me. We rely so heavily upon your help with our work, and we value you greatly!

Dawn Henderson of Austin Design Works—wow! You've made your mark on my career. Thank you for a gorgeous new website and stunning branding. I feel like a new *me*!

Special thanks to Judy Peterson, Shannon Wright, Meagan Cook, Erin Engelhard, Kara Beck, Marge Burke, and Connie VanderBeek: thank you for your friendship and constant encouragement. Girlfriends like you are a rare treasure! Same goes to my writerly gals—thank you, ladies! Cindy, Jan, Pam, Kay, Lee, Charity, Mel, Rachael, Gigi... the list goes on!

My advance reader team: thank you for being my first

readers and the ones who help get my stories to the public. You all rock! And Bromke's Bookworms—thank you for your unending kindness to me!

Mom and Dad—thank you for all of your help these last couple years. Every bit of it has made a huge difference to me (and Ed and Eddie). Love you!

Ed and Eddie—you know this. Always for you! I love you both! Winnie, too!